The Opium Emporium
Rising

Casanova Da Vinci

Copyright © 2017 Casanova Da Vinci

All rights reserved.

ISBN- 10: 1539985814
ISBN-13: 978-1539985815

DEDICATION

It is sometimes hard to imagine a world without Touch, Smell or Sensation; vested in many abilities that we all share a common interest in together as a Society, not to mention as a singular unit: Woman and Man. Without such people as The Explorer, The Womanizer, The Romantic, The Poet, or The Love Seeker, the Human Race would be in one big pickle. They are the ones who lift another person's imagination, arouse their thoughts, trigger attraction, and bring into effect things that can only be described as Magical!

Without people – Human Beings – we are led to believe that "Love", not mistaking this for "True Love", will cease to exist! One the other hand, our own observations on the animal kingdom and their behavior, brings that question to "How do we succeed in making 'Love' survive, forever?" The answer still, will remain: We cannot.

I would like to thank everyone who helped me gather research and factual depictions that created "The Bordello Tales Collection", and for supporting me through the years.

 For Danielle La Grande – My Muse

CONTENTS

Acknowledgments   *i*

1 The Opium Emporium   *1*

INTRODUCTION

For more than 300 years, the two towns that border Yorkshire's borders of North and East: Evermore and Borello, have been at war; through each generation since the very first in the late 1700's, to present, both families have been taught by their peers to hate their neighbors, while all the while during countless battles, something has caused a great change in each their retaliations.

For the Duchess of Evermore, Lady Melissa Ellington-Evermore, the present day changes in her family have led to the death of her youngest niece, Carrie Brindley-White.

Lady Evermore's husband, Lord David Evermore, the last remaining Evermore, is too saddened to bury his niece, because he is inconsolably troubled to find that her death was through no accident, but murder.

In Borello, Lady Mallandra Gruber, the land owner of Borello and all of its houses and businesses, comes head to head with the hands that deal fate. And from "Evermore" to the dark, seedy confines of "The Quarter", love, passion, lust and depravity may well conquer all within the adult erotic stories of The Bordello Tales.

'Love gained, Love lost, Tragedy'

1 THE OPIUM EMPORIUM

The Saunders Institute scandal had been ended more than eighteen months before I staggered into Borello with nothing but the clothes I stood in and the scars of my detention. For all of this time I had no recollection of where or who I was with, or indeed if I'd had been anywhere other than unconscious. The Square was packed, but not too packed not to see an almost broken man collapse before them. Between my semi-conscious state I was beginning to wonder if I was just lucky in the fact that Michael had returned from his prison in America; the last place on earth that he would ever go back to, while within the confines of Borello House, Lady Gruber's heart was finally melted; the return of the only one man in the world who could have fixed her broken spirit after the cold blooded murder of her lover, Tristan Lazenby – a potential victim of forbidden love it was said behind closed doors of Evermore, and even in very close quarters of Borello House, too.

Michael was the one who found me before the Borello police did, which was a good gesture, but certainly not a good move – I knew all about the torrid Alice Gruber and Michael Slattery Affair that had begun after he left Redstone University.

'***Alice will have you killed!***' I gasped.

Michael did not flinch or falter from picking me up into his strong wide arms and carry me to an apartment in the East Square Tenement's, all the while nodding and greeting all of those who greeted him with a smile. Once we were safely inside the silently dark apartment he bumped against a light switch that had the whole room illuminate; brightly colored walls, picture frames, posters and immaculate furniture waited for my body to be rested down on the giant leather sofa that beckoned me to its gentle embrace.

Making sure that I was settled, he checked my eyes with a roaming arc-like swirling finger that waved in front of my face.

'Well, it's not concussion at least. You look like hell!' He assured me that my head was okay of any serious injury, before raising his tone to demand I tell him of some attacker he believed assaulted me.

I looked at him with a cold stare that showed both my fear and an overwhelming fail to hold back the pain.

'I'll get you something for those wounds.' Michael declared walking off into what I presumed was the kitchen. The wall which separated both rooms was hollowed out, so that through the hole I was able to see him walk up to a cupboard and quickly take out a First Aid box and a small bowl that he filled at the sink with fresh clean water.

'You need me...'

'Yes, Lucas,' Michael interrupted suddenly crouching down in front of me at the sofa with the dish filled with water and the First Aid box opened. 'I need you to get better. I'm going to ask you a couple of questions, Okay? Now, this is going to be difficult for you...'

My thoughts were excromocated, strewn and mixed up like I had never known. The hypnotic tones of my heart beat had me down my head to the pillow, while all I could think in my head was that I would be the perfect trophy win for The Gruber's.

'You want to know the secrets of Evermore?' I replied in a strained voice that had him rush away and get me some drinking water in a large glass tumbler.

Telling me to drink it slowly, I sipped a few drops before I gently pushed the glass away from me coughing at the sting that caught the back of my dried up throat.

'The Institute really played a number on you, my friend.'

'And are you, Michael – *A friend?*' I whispered.

His answer did not come as I had expected. 'Yes, we are all friends here now. You have to rest, I will bring a Doctor...'

The word alone made me physically shake from head to foot.

'Alright, it's alright, it's a friend who is a Doctor, she will be able to help you. Don't worry, the Institute is no more, Lucas, you are safe here with us. I promise.'

It was a promise that Michael would live to regret.

Leaving me alone in the apartment for a short time he told me to make myself at home, while he left to find his Doctor friend, Sylvie Harper and bring her back to see to me. In the meantime, I rested, then rested some more, until eventually I couldn't rest anymore; the hours turned into points of concern, worry and all of a sudden fear. The pictures unleashed behind my eyes were unbearable, sick and vile. My time inside the "Hell Cells" of The Saunders Institute had been of pain, torture and the most perverted experiments performed on my body; the scars below my neck and back showing very clearly the healed wounds of cuts, incisions and skin grafts. I didn't know how many operations I'd had, or how much of my blood had spilt out onto those illegal Operating Room floors. But what I did know, was that I was finally out and that I was alive.

Gentleman Or Thief?

With frequent visits from Michael and Doctor Harper over the passing months of my healing process, I began to gain back my mobility and strength to defend myself in any time of trouble. In his spare time away from Borello House, both Michael and I would spar with one another, wrestle and even sword fight to have me at my best. Still, I didn't know why he saved me in The Square that day, and still I waited for him telling me the real reason behind his defiance against The Gruber's – Alice especially.

'How are you feeling now? I thought a walk into Borello may help you get your confidence back?' Michael suggested.

The whole idea of walking out of that apartment door and into a place that may well reject me was surfacing fast to my objecting tone, until I had a single thought in my mind that spoke something completely different and most surprising – **Elizabeth!**

Michael stepped back suddenly. 'Is that who you came back to Borello for, Lucas, Elizabeth?'

I nodded as he started to rub away at his chin. 'Then it shall be Elizabeth that we go and see.'

He said this with quite a happy delivery of character, one which found me surprised. '***Go see Elizabeth!***'

His very much abrupt pause in glee had him return to me with a look of knowing, though Michael's lack of interest in knowing more about me did bring no end of apologies.

'You want a woman right? Well, if there is one thing in Borello that a man really needs, then it's in The Bordello…'

'*Elizabeth is a prostitute?*' I gasped with awe.

It was at this moment that Michael knew he had mistaken my needs as some silent call for a common paid whore to tend me.

'Apologies, Lucas, I wasn't thinking straight…'

I excused him – this once – by default, of course. Though this was at the time seen as a huge setback in our strange friendship, we were just able to move on. And on we did, into Borello Town.

He showed me all the places, both of trading and residential, unbeknowing that for so long I once haunted the streets, rooftops and those out of the way places of the town before being sent away to die in a clinic that served slow death – as far as I was aware, that was.

'Doctor Harper says you'll be almost one-hundred percent by the end of the week, hopefully, have you got any plans?' He asked grabbing out at a fruit cart and taking two red apples.

'Here, start right in the day and keep the Doctor away.'

Taking the apple from him I tried to find the right answer in which to reply, it was hard enough only just coming out of the apartment into the town. Maybe my hesitation would have sufficed a temporary 'Step back', but it didn't.

'Come on, I'll treat you to breakfast at The Bastion, it's not that far from here. Then you can tell me of your plans when your back on your feet again.'

And that was that. We walked the short way to The Bastion and entered the Tavern like there was nothing to stop us from doing so. At first the Landlady looked up, and then the locals.

'*Michael!*' Molly Cooper the sultry looking Landlady cried out with suspicion.

Michael told me to go and find a table while he went to speak with the Landlady, who was beginning to look none too sure about either of us coming into her establishment.

'The Lexicon Rule, Michael, have you forgotten it already?' She growled out at him with desperation and sincerity.

'Molly, come on, he's a family friend, don't be like this.' Michael appealed to her better side, though to be honest she didn't look to me like she had one – ever.

'***Incognito!*** ' She exclaimed indicating two fingers flicking from her eyes to his and mine, clearly indicating that she was keeping an eye us both.

Michael looked at me now sitting down at an empty table.

'Incognito…and a round for the house,' he smiled.

Molly nodded and began to pull a pint of ale. 'That'll do nicely. Just remember where you are?'

The time spent with this man who was no other than the lover and soon to be husband of Lady Alice Gruber, whipped up my curiosity. He was at best interesting, though his very nature itself became fascinating.

'You'll find we're all friends here, Lucas, so tell me, what ***are*** your plans?'

The repeated question had not gone from the forefront of my mind, it had been answered already through a hundred reasons already that had flooded my brain whilst making our way to the Tavern through the town.

'Can I trust you?' I asked, knowing only too well that Michael was just like anyone else. 'With a secret, I mean?'

'Well, I can't guarantee it won't be tortured out of…***Shit!*** Hey, I'm sorry, I didn't mean to…'

Michael was embarrassed by his lack of tact. 'It's fine. Really, it's fine. Borello has changed so much since I've been gone, does the old church still stand by The Bell Tower?'

I guess it was an opportune moment, something that would lighten the blow of the secret in which I was to tell. Surprised as he may have been at first, too, the facts of my identity in Borello Town previous to my return made him laugh out very loudly in an exaggerated tone of disbelief – or denial.

'You mock me, Michael?' I cried.

He began waving his hands in front of me. 'Of course not.'

'Then why the laughter, friend?'

Shifting forward in his seat Michael waved me closer.

'The Hood was a man of code and honor and spunk, not a man...excuse me for my insensitivity, Lucas, but that is definitely not you. The treatments from The Institute...'

Did Michael see me as someone who didn't have these very same habits, traits and values as The Hood, or was this some attempt to have me explain myself more clearly? Either he was goading a reaction, or he was merely dismissing the idea of Borello's most mysterious Night Hunter because it was dangerous for me to claim.

'Then he is still here...The Hood?' I exclaimed heartedly.

Michael shushed me. 'Keep your voice down, Lucas, do you want everyone to hear you? That name we no longer use around here in Borello, my friend.'

I quickly calmed myself down and apologized to an immediate acceptance of a slow raised hand and brashed winked smile.

Molly brought us our drinks and some food to the table while stopping at a nearby table where two occupants, a couple of women pointing at us as if asking who we were. Molly whispered before continuing on her way with the food.

'Anything we have to worry about, Molly?' Michael asked.

'That depends, your friend is causing quite a stir with the ladies around here, they wanted to know how much you charge for the hour, Kid!' She replied as though considering asking the very same question herself after a brief roaming of her eyes upon me, the dilated excitement of her findings pleasing.

Michael laughed to himself. 'Tell them he charges...'

I threw myself at him. 'Hey, what are you doing?'

I was not happy with his sudden choice of humor.

'Relax, it's just a bit of fun,' he was quick to come to his own defense. 'Tell them...a hundred for the hour, one-fifty if he can take them both!'

Molly was suddenly surprised. '**Seriously!** He looks like he needs more than a Sheekan's Lunch to get his dick up!'

Michael gave her a disgusted look that had her shrug her shoulders and give a very mischievous smile before returning back to the women's table to give them the offer. While she

The Opium Emporium: Rising

was away, I told Michael that I was looking for someone who was last seen here in Borello.

'I would hazard a guess and say it is that Elizabeth girl you were asking about earlier?' He said not once breaking his stare from the two women who were soft waving to us both.

Returning to our table Molly gave a smile. 'They said go fuck yourselves, the Kid is only worth fifty at best.'

Michael seemed disappointed that the two women had turned me down like they did, as for me, I didn't care that much about the whole joke he was playing. Maybe I should have channeled a lot deeper in my mind to find those instinctive feelings to notice that Michael's fast decline in temperament would lead to the death of two women later that same evening. Their bodies mutilated beyond recognition, cut to pieces and displayed across half a mile of Evermore dry seed land. Of course this was not where they had been killed.

Stopping Michael with the pushing of ale before him, I had in a slightly convincing manner distracted him from the other table and finally found his full and undivided attention.

'The way molly looks at you!' I exclaimed cryptically.

His eyes seemed to hover in the air as if looking at something, but all the same looking at nothing. He heard the statement and yet, with no other show of expression except for a low smile, he wiped the remnants of froth from his lips.

'It's complicated, Lucas, as is are all things to do with this damned town! Listen, I know all I need to know about you and that…well, let's just say, I know the story so far. As for me on the other hand…'

'Would it soften the blow any easier if I was to tell you that I, too, know much about you?' I replied between a short sipping of my ale and a raised eyebrow.

Michael was not so impressed by the bold statement, but he was certainly in favor of building up his kept laughter at the way that I presented it to him.

'In a couple of weeks, I will be Master to Lord of Borello House, it's residences, businesses and Houses, so help me god! There is nothing more to know about me than the obvious, and even that, my friend, is a little loosened on facts.'

His marriage to Lady Alice Gruber would indeed bring him the title of such an honoree position of Lord, though the sovereign laws of the land would deny him any true status. He knew it and so did I, as well as any other privy mind in Resheen.

'The Houses will not yield to your rule as some would like!'

'And that is where you are wrong! I don't intend to have my town yield to me, I intend them to have hope in a future where they only have to yield to their own demons and flaws. I will bring freedom to Borello, or I'll die trying. I am hoping that we can become great allies, Lucas, you're House and my House.'

The suggestion alone was bulleted in the guise of "Surprise", and then some. Allies against scores of other Houses that would see Borello burn, rather than allow its reputation to fall unto the cascades of simplicity. Chaos had reigned too heavily on the town for it to change its ways now.

'Do you remember Xander O'Neill, a Cousin of mine from a House near Seacliffe? He once told me, if I wanted to gain from nothing a better reputation, then all I had to do was stop and listen to the people's voices. For his actions seen as hostile against the dozen Houses, he was killed, tortured and maimed for standing in the way of the cruelest son-of-a-bitch this side of The Rift. Your crusade is flawed, but only by default of your secondary status. We are Assassin's, Michael, living among the dead who would rather end their suffering and pain by less harsh means, than to be witness to depravity and evilness.'

He listened all the way through without as much as a blink.

'Lord London and his men did not have the blessing of any House, not when he tried stopping your Cousin, anyway. In my case, I have no contenders, no enemies, and certainly no Lords from The Baker's Dozen wanting to kill me. It is by Royal appointment that I take my place upon Borello, not by instructions of The Machine that drives Evermore and its puppets…! Fuck! Hey, I'm sorry, Lucas!'

He apologized for what seemed like the thousandth time in one day, something that was quickly becoming a habit for him. I was calm, maybe because of the ale going straight to my head, or maybe because I believed that Michael's heart was in his town, the people and the belief that one day it would become free of all outside influences. The outburst meant nothing except for the truth that he felt inside him.

'Unlike those of my so-called family, Melissa, I see no such Majesty in Evermore. I believe allies is not something that the Houses would expect, but then, I believe they would never allow it to happen, either.' I returned a fact that had him in a fit of drunken desperation finding the words to reply.

The moment was gone. 'Let's get out of here, before we get ourselves in Molly's bad books. I can say, it's better to be on her good side than in the way of her punches!'

Laughing as we stood and plotted our walk to the door we were stopped by a man, middle aged, rough and drawn looking as if he'd been travelling some distance.

'Lord Lucas, I apologize for this rude intrusion, but I must speak with you and Master Slattery at once!' He whispered up quietly before us. 'News from a mutual confirms that The Houses are in disrepute, as are others around Chatandra. My message brings only bad news I'm afraid.'

The Houses, four in all within Resheen and its outer borders, while more than three hundred more around the world looked on in pandemonium as the founding axis of power began to teeter on collapse. There were – and still are – more ways than any to begin such a move, the only thing, of course, was that no matter who pushed the button to begin the sequence of all present and future actions. They would find no peace in the spoils of their crimes against The Sanctum of The Order.

The man left as soon as he had delivered the message, his own well-being in threat of being hanged as a traitor, if not just simply a trespasser entering an unstable town.

After leaving The Bastille Tavern, we made our way to The Bell Tower, once here Michael pointed up to the top of the steeple where an open window stood half open.

'Rumor has it that The Hood used The Bell Tower as his hideout, though this is just rumor, of course. His work was not alone, it is also claimed. He was once a savior of this town,

Lucas...'

'**Savior!** But you said...'

'I said his name is no longer mentioned, which is true if you don't wish Alice to discover your secret. It is hard to believe, but I knew as soon as I saw you in The Square that you were him.' Michael made no fuss in letting me know he knew the truth about my alter-ego – The Borello Hood.

I had no idea what he was talking about when referring to The Hood in the way that he did, except for the small fragments that my tired mind processed now and again. I was becoming weaker, colder with the refirmation of my healing and the power of the high dosage drugs that were slowly leaving my blood system.

'Here, let me help you find a seat.' Michael looked around for something for me to rest upon and gather my strength. 'Here, sit down and wait here, I'll be back in a moment.'

He disappeared quickly from my sight to enter The Bell Tower, before he did, as he said he would, he returned a few moments later with a hoodie, pair of boots and shirt.

'Here, put these on...be quick, we don't want to be seen.' He advised me checking that the way was clear.

When I was dressed he told me to follow him through the town to a part which was very much off of the beaten track – Dragon Town.

Dragon Town Express

It was a forgotten small part of town on the edge of Borello, its population small, and yet prepared for any sudden hostilities against its people. It boasted more than eight hundred homes, apartments and other places that tenants called Home.

'Have you ever been here before, Lucas?' He asked as if half expecting the answer to be "Yes", but the answer being a definite "No", simply to the fact I had heard of 'Dragon Town' just never had any reason to come here.

Michael introduced me to Raymond, one of the House Seers;

the head of an exclusive household that offered the very best in entertainment and leisure, including hard drugs that had many attendees hooked on coming back for more, until finally overdosing or being executed for one reason or another – mainly that of bad debt, sometimes by Contract. It was a harsh place that had many harsh customs, rules and laws.

'Stay close, Kid, don't wander off in here.' He warned me.
From the very moment of entering the tall steel gates that separated the community from those of Borello, I was greeted with naked women who were trying to negotiate prices for a fuck, hand job, blow job, even a threesome, if I wanted to get kinky. The tone was low, but what people said they meant.

'The woman there on the right, that's Carina Del Marriere, you need to talk with her. Offer her fifteen, she'll take ten, but you need to get her quick before those guys over there do!' Michael said dropping his stare to a young woman with a limp in her step, before changing his glancing direction over to a small group of five twenty-something men.
Calling the woman over Michael did the negotiating, and as he had predicted she agreed to take ten. As soon as an agreement was made we were taken to a small apartment of hers where she began to undress me – this was not part of the deal! A few moments after getting into Carina's place Michael came walking through the door and introduced himself.

'*I ain't got any money!* ' Carina piped up worried and believing that it was a robbery.

'This is Lucas, he is looking for a beautiful woman that calls herself Elizabeth.' He announced to the woman's sudden strange, if not weird reaction.

'*Elizabeth!*' She gasped. 'Elizabeth Spinks, you mean?'
Carina seemed to know Elizabeth, or at the very least, she knew of her full title.

'Can you tell me where she is?' I asked with a surge of uncontainable excitement that was bursting from my voice and seemingly scaring the woman.

'I'm sorry for your loss Kid, Elizabeth Spinks died just a few months ago there, she was right as rain one day and then the next…!'

Michael stopped the woman with a gentle hand resting on her shoulder, the look of needing time alone with me showing in his face. Carina nodded silently and then made her way out of the room. Stopping her momentarily Michael handed her some money to compensate for the time and keep silent the incident.

'You knew her, didn't you?' I said dreamily, taking in the news of what the prostitute had just told me. 'You knew her?'

Michael rose his head. 'Yes. Yes, I did. I'm sorry, but I had to make sure that it was by other means you found out, do you understand?'

There was a visible rage that Michael recognized in me which had him hold out his arms and lift up his chin to me. 'I deserve…!'

Really, do you really think that a man who has fought hell itself to come back and find his one true love dead, isn't going to avenge anything that held the essence of Elizabeth Spinks' name, or memory? Wake up, this man who claims to be my friend kept from me the one thing that was keeping me together – now I was unhinged.

The first punch that I gave out to Michael's face was hard enough to put him on his arse, whereas the second was met by his large hand that flipped me over onto my back – I was taken by surprise. I was down, but not out.

'Your attack is sloppy, Lucas!' Michael stated as he stood ready against me. 'Try again!'

There I was on my arse with the thought of kicking his, but in my spirit I felt nothing but resistance to my calls to get up and carry out the simple command. I couldn't move.

Michael put down a hand to pull me up off of the floor, my refusal making him break his stance and turn away while I struggled to my feet. He turned back and gave a strained smile.

'What the fuck happened in that place, Lucas?' He asked as if dreading to know the answer.

Maybe I would have told him everything, if I could have trusted him a little more than what I did. But with Michael, he had already made his very first mistake by lying to me about

Elizabeth, my private life was none of his business.

'***They killed me!*** ' I replied, making my way out of the apartment back into the Borello streets.

The Den Of Gentlemen

Michael's continued apology for his lengthy silence brought me to accept his invitation to attend The Castle Keep, a Gentleman's Club that catered for all manner of clientele, including privacy to smoke opium and consort with other, more exclusive residents and visitors to Borello.

The Club was huge, the building pre-1800's, its architecture of the most exquisite quality and detail; gargoyles standing on the lip of its high roof, angels and cherubs facing one another in rows of eight, while above the main entrance door an insignia that was at least ten feet in width and just as much in height stood baring the name: The Castle Keep.

'What is this place…***Masons?*** ' I found myself asking him as we entered the hallway where Michael was warmly relieved of his coat by a half-naked woman.

His response was quick, silent almost, but clear.

'Here, we don't talk about such things, Lucas. Come, follow me, I want to introduce you to someone.' He said before leading the way through a long corridor that seemed never ending, wide and darkly lit with what looked like old gas lamps. Everything in that building gave an odor, not a distasteful one, but one that you would get from old wood, layers of polish and cleaning substances. The marble floor clicked as we walked over it, the squeaking of our shoes echoing around us until we came to a stop, or rather Michael did first.

'One question, have you ever been high?'

I was in two minds with the thought of two separate questions: Have I ever been high up in the air? And then, have I ever been high out of my face on drugs? The answer to these was easy and most definitely yes, but I doubted Michael would have known no difference in what came back as a confirmation.

'Yes,' I replied watching his hand turning the handle and push open the door for me to enter.

Walking inside I was greeted with a wall of excess smoke from the many people sat around walls, silver oak tables and on soft leather sofas and chairs taking in and exhaling opium. The pipes tall, the bowls wide, while each bubbly pipe tail-like extension was taken in hand by several people who breathed in its intoxicating dense smoke of Elixir.

'This shit is good,' a man easily in his fifties informed me as he rolled back his eyes and submerged himself into an hallucinogenic trip that would take away his troubles – or so he and others like him believed the illicit narcotic did by magic.

Michael had found us both a seat near the center of the room, by his side a small group of city men, their dress was all suit and shiny shoes. Shouting over he told me sit down and have a drink – Brandy.

'I don't drink,' I told him.

'Then a toke, perhaps…or don't you smoke either?' He smiled passing me a tail from a nearby bubbly pipe sitting on the table right in front of us.

Taking a hold of the end I pushed it between my lips before taking in a deep toke of the smoke from the bong-style vessel. The opium filled my lungs, senses, worming its way through my system and bringing me to slump back in my soft comfortable seat. Its power of intoxication brought the lids of my eyes heavy, too heavy to keep open, as slowly I began my descent into the opium enriched dreamscape.

Still sensing Michael by the side of me, I latched onto his voice. He was talking to the man across from him; The voices mingled out of context, reassembled themselves, and then they were gone. Adsensed to the point of no return I started to drift into a fantastical and wondrous interlude of a Self-Fulfilling Prophecy long since forgotten.

Inside my subconscious I was floating; by the feel of the air it was breezy, while by my sides I started to see wooden beams, then a lake of water that pulled my body along with the current. Fish of all shapes and sizes danced across the water, their fins looking sharp and dangerous as they glided their skimming bodies around me. The water, too, rising and dropping with sequential waves of whites, blues and greens in a crashing crescendo of bright rainbow colors.

I was in a world of fantasy: A world within a world. It was once a dangerous place…what if it still was? My gaze upon the strange colorful sky had me fascinated; the rolls of blue merging themselves into purple, crimson and gold. Clouds puffed up, then they deflated as if in time to my very own heartbeat, before they separated to bring forward a face…familiar – Elizabeth!

'You shouldn't have come here,' she whispered as a horse in flames rode past her to disappear inside the expanding clouds.

'I had to come back…to…'

The moment I began to talk to her she disappeared, just like the horse that seemed to slow down and look at me before it made its way into the reddening sky. I could not see Elizabeth anymore. She was gone.

An overwhelming feeling filled me; both with the intoxication from the opium and Brandy that Michael force-fed me stirred my adrenaline, the sheer strength of the drug bringing me to a baseline of slow motion sounds and images, while correlated abuse from both substances forced me to close my eyes and fall into an unwilling unconsciousness. I was out for the count – literally.

Land Of The Living

Michael had seen to it that I was taken back to his Apartment in Borello, while he attended an engagement with Lady Gruber – Alice, who he had not talked about much since our paths crossed. But, as the day drew to a close of daylight, he returned to the apartment and told me to get myself ready.

'There's a ball tonight.' He announced making his way into the bedroom and picking out a pile of clothes that he threw over to me, one by one he looked out something that would be fitting for such an invitation; first the shirt, then the trousers, until finally he stopped and looked at me standing there.

'What is it? What's wrong?'

'A ball…you mean like a…'

'Masquerade Ball, yeah, so hurry up and get into them.'

The trousers were of a soft thin black leather, the white shirt of woven silk that touched my skin with soothing comfort. A pair of cufflinks and a cravat for final measure made me look with a new built pride in the mirror, something that did not go unnoticed to Michael.

'There you are?' He cried walking over and slapping my back.

Ready to attend the Masquerade Ball, we left the apartment as soon as it was dark enough to walk the streets safely to Borello House. It didn't take us long as the whole town was almost deserted of people.

'Are you and Alice…I mean Lady Gruber…'

Michael shushed me suddenly. 'Put this on.'

From behind his back he took out a mask; blue in color with a gold tease of embossed lines that held every so often a cubic zirconia that sparkled in the limited light outside the grounds of the house.

'What about you?' I asked him, just as he took out another mask from his inside jacket pocket; the merry down peach surface of the mask became broken with the ripple effect of reds, oranges and fiery waves that brought a central need to look at the eyes.

'I like it.' I whispered showing a hand for him to continue.

Inside the house of Borello, I found the rooms at the rear quite strange, though this was through my comparing the whole construct of the House to Evermore, a habit I had formed some two or three months after first finding my fake identity in the town.

'This door will take you into the Main Hall where they are having the Ball. Now, do you remember the plan?' He spoke up as if I did indeed know what the plan was – but there was no plan. 'I'm only kidding. Right, let's get our masks on and get inside. Stay close to me.'

Michael laughed briefly at the little joke that he had made, and then without any further delay we both entered The Main Hall; it's large floor filling out eight hundred feet of space, each wall spanning a hundred and thirty feet, and a ceiling very much like the one I had idolized as a child back at Evermore. It was as grand as any other stately home I'd seen.

'Mingle…Make friends…Have fun.' Michael smiled while being grabbed around the neck by two very young beautiful women, their identity hidden by the ivy green masks that gave them an alluring feminine look.

A couple of seconds later and Michael had disappeared, taken into the large crowd of gatherers who slowly danced to the enchanting music of Graham Stokes' Only The Love. Standing back I took my place beside a line of people that weren't dancing, some who were waiting for the right person to come along and ask them, while others I'm sure were timing they're quick getaway by humble excuse.

The music sounded out into the hall, feet moved in unison while at the height of the chorus, hands reached up and descended into those of their partners in the dance. Women tilted their heads, glanced around to pick one man, one woman from the crowd, before finally swooning down upon them with a lunge into their arms. I, too, had the unfortunate honor of having a woman drop into my arms and gaze up at me with the strangest of smiles.

'I'm sorry, I don't dance,' I informed her, but still she kept smiling at me – did she know who I was?

Taking a hold of my hand the woman led me onto the dancefloor of the Hall and began to guide me; almost like dancing but with a short step that had me almost tripping over the young woman's feet.

'You are not enjoying yourself!' She exclaimed stopping still and placing her hands on her hips. 'Maybe we both need some fresh air and a break from all of this?'

The suggestion alone was good enough for me.

We left the Hall and made our way to the veranda doors that had been posted a Servant holding freshly poured champagne, wine and other, stronger alcoholic cocktails.

'Champagne?' She asked picking up two glasses.

Accepting the drink we walked through the doors and onto the wide veranda where we sat on a nearby hammock together, just in case it went too far back for either one of us to topple. Finally we were sat comfortably looking up at the cloudless night sky.

'So, what brings you back to Borello?' She asked quite suddenly and innocently.

The question was not vague, more outright and questionable in itself as to the sense of the initial enquiry.

'Excuse me…I mean…'

'Yes, we have, many times!' She replied before I could readjust to the previous misspoken question.

'We have?' I answered with a "Wow" look on my face.

The young woman rolled into me, cuddling into the base of my side and wrapping a warm, gentle arm around the front of my waist. It was almost as though she thought of me as someone I was not.

'Your perfume, it smells familiar,' I whispered softly.

The young woman's hand around my waist began to rub up against me, her breath panting across my silk covered chest, as her other free hand roamed and dithered around the top of my leg in circles of eight.

'They say people only come back to Borello for two things, one is obvious, it gives them cause to put right the wrongs they were given. The second…more permanent. You came back to find the one thing that you can't have!'

Though I wanted to ask the young woman questions, my lack of energy restricted my movement, until eventually I had fallen into a relaxing unconscious state that had me waking to a stein of ale being poured over my face to wake me.

'*What the…!*' I yelped opening my eyes to see Michael and the two women that had abducted him earlier all at once towering over me.

'Steady old boy, don't move too quickly.' He advised, jumping down next to me, followed by one of the women who landed heavily on his knee. The hammock trembled and shook.

'What time is it?' I asked to the objections of the women.

'Too early in the morning to finish the party.' One cried out lowering herself down and kissing Michael full on the lips.

Michael was in fine spirits with the girls, the booze and of course the opium, too. As for me, I was getting a strange kind of thirst in my mouth, one which would not be doused or quenched by ale alone.

'*I need...I need!*' I suddenly couldn't remember.

'You need a good woman my friend, and tonight, you shall have one.' Michael cried out grabbing a hold of the woman on his knee and helping her get off of him.

The thought that Michael had gotten me a prostitute was the closest thing to my mind with his words that were sounding strangely like an echo; as if under water, or inside a tunnel of sorts – or both – I was baked.

Nodding to one of the girls he pointed over to a bar at the far side of the veranda from where we were sat.

'Brandy. Brandy will fix you up, it always does.'

He was right, the alcohol from the expensive looking bottle took away the dry parched feeling from my mouth and throat. It was now that Michael passed me a Corsican Spot Pipe, its contents hidden by a carefully designed cover that allowed the opium ball to burn successively and release intensely into the Tokers lungs with tremendous speed. A few seconds later and I was glancing around, looking up and swaying to and fro.

'Feel better?' He asked filling up my glass again.

From being tired and exhausted I became filled with a 'Must', but I was not sure what 'Must' it was that I needed to do, I turned to the young woman at the side of me and smiled.

'I think I need to do something!' I said, suddenly bursting out into a fit of laughter. It was obvious the opium was now free-wheeling around my body; through every vein, every nerve, every blood cell that was not an antibody against the toxic high. I felt fantastic – almost.

'*A party!*' The woman answered looking at Michael and prompting him to speak up.

'A party may just do it, you know, loosen you up a little more. Then there's your surprise that I have for you, too, so don't go start making a fucking arse of yourself, do you hear?' He laughed with a hidden sincere warning in his tone.

Pointing in the direction of the door we all left and flooded back out into the streets of Borello, where as clear as it was, I had conquered my fear of venturing out into the world. To be honest, my mind didn't feel as if it belonged to me, so really I didn't give a shit – Tonight, I was invincible.

Shades Of Rhythm

Strutting through the doors of Borello's top nightclub – The Angel – both Michael and I were stopped by two of the most burley of Bouncers I'd seen, and they were not looking too happy by our arrival. The two women from the party left our sides, their own way took them straight inside where without pause in their step they disappeared into the crowd.

'Evening Lads, you out for a good night then?' The first Bouncer, a little shorter in height than his associate laughed at us. 'Are you together?'

This laughable statement went unnoticed to Michael, but for me, it was a lot more personal. It burned me inside.

'Actually, we're with them!' Michael pointed forward and passed the two laughing men.

At first my gaze upon the two women was relaxed, filled with that of unsurities as to who they were, until I happened to see a very unique and familiar brooch around one of the women's necks. It's Mother of Pearl filled center, while around its gold enclosure the motif of Cassiopeia.

'Now, if you'll excuse us, we have Ladies to attend to.' Michael informed the Bouncers, who then stood aside for us to pass and make our way over to the women.

'Lucas, may I introduce…'

'*I was in The Square!*' Lady Harriot Sycamore exclaimed with a raised smile directed at me. 'You are the man that

Michael found and helped are you not?'
Turning to Michael I noticed he had a look of puzzlement, just as much as I was unaware of the woman seeing me that day, so was he. We both had to now tread very carefully.

'Were we pissed as Newts and just as steady on our feet?' Michael turned the whole awkward moment into a joke and began laughing out loudly. The two women, seeing that he was laughing joined in too, until Lady Sycamore stopped suddenly.

'Actually, no, you were injured,' she said glancing a nod at me. 'It was in the morning, you will remember it well, because it was the day that Lady Gruber chewed one of Michael's balls off for being…Now, how did she put?'
Michael knew exactly what they said, or rather, what Alice had said to him that same morning. The woman had Michael at a disadvantage; she knew many things about him and me, but our secret or safeguard of that knowledge was unsure.

'What do you want?' I spoke up dryly, taking the woman by the arm and escorting her forcefully into the club.
Harriot struggled, for a few moments before settling down.

'What makes you think I want anything?' She replied just as dryly with a hint of anger in her tone.
The odds were that when someone had information that was considered highly valuable, then more often than not they were in a position to barter the price of their silence.

'The morning I came to Borello…'
'The morning you came back to Borello, you mean?' She came to interrupt with an annoyance that boiled my blood.

'Are you a school teacher, Lady Sycamore?' I asked.
She gave a shy smile that was quickly followed by a "No".

'Then please refrain from interrupting me! When I…returned to Borello that morning, you saw me and Michael…'
Michael pulled on my shoulder. '**Lucas, we have to leave!**'
Harriot shook her head from side to side. 'You won't get far, the guards outside have surrounded the place, not to mention the two dozen Borello Police Officers that are standing around you in here. So, unless you know some magical spell that can make you both disappear, then I'd say you're ***screwed!***'

This was an unusual state of affairs; the locksonet of the past that had saved me of the death sentence from my own Cousin, Lady Melissa Ellington-Evermore, now became a mediocre mess that could well have spelt my end – as both Master Lucas Cavendish and The Borello Hood.

'Do you like magic, Lady Sycamore?' I asked with a piercing glare that burned deep into her eyes.

Before she could answer I noticed a glint – yes, it was definitely a glint that glimmered a shard of her very soul; the eyes being the one true access to anyone's human side was by way of the eyes. There were no exceptions.

'I really don't…think this is…*I love magic tricks!* ' She spoke ill intendedly at first, but then her tone shallowed to a wayward excitement which had her friend Lady Valerie Dobrev throw her a look of wonder.

'What if I could make everyone in this whole room disappear, except us, would that be a magic trick worthy enough of your attention…and maybe your help?'

Michael gave me an unsure look, a gaze of caution and an even stronger look of preparing for the worst. His knowledge of me as The Hood was vague, though the techniques in which Michael himself had used just a few years previous on Lady Gruber was still fresh in his mind to realize that my intentions were to be proven.

'That would be wonderful…I mean, such a great trick has one very curious of the outcome. You are very…!'

I moved closer to Harriot, my hand brushing gently over her shoulder as if to guide her into a turn, before standing very close behind her, my face near to her ear so as I could whisper.

'See those lights Harriot, the ones that dance and shine in your lost and lonely eyes?'

Harriot was looking uncomfortable, but not at all in a way of turning back to me and disrupting my plan of completing the task; to swoon her off of her feet and bring her around to the fact that by personal, pleasurable and intimate association of such a villain as I, she would be whipped beyond the call of consciousness to revoke her statement made to both Michael

and me that evening. Would it work? I didn't know, my whole body seemed different after escaping The Saunders' Institute.
Placing a gentle hand around her waist I leant further into the nape of her neck, my feathering kisses onto the naked skin had her moan and rest back her head onto my waiting shoulder.

'The lights are beautiful, like diamonds almost, wouldn't you agree?' I whispered softly, again, my kisses hovered around the nape of her neck, as with a quickening turn of her to face me, she looked straight into my eyes – directly into my eyes that were now scanning, searching and needing to find that one short glimmer that would expose Harriot to The Tremadale; a once enriched way of communication between ancient Far East Tribes. Known to them as The Tremadale, better known to the rest of us Westerner's as The Language of Love.

'We wait for a moment to pass us by, and yet, we do not take the opportunity to introduce it…do you see it, Harriot?'
Harriot's heart was beating fast, her eyes lost in my eyes, her mouth falling agape and her body beginning to sway side to side. The music was vibrant, steady in its bassline, while that of a melodic overture was soothing to both that of Harriot's and my ears. Alas, however, I was not the prisoner of its rhythmatic beats, nor that of a fever pitched thirst that only lust, pleasure and unbound sexual intensity could fix. Harriot was at The Carvott stage; to her the whole place would be completely empty of people, except for me – The Carvott Speaker
Leaning her head closer to mine she kissed my lips with a short peck at first, and then with a wider arch about her mouth we kissed deeply, passionately and more intensely than most people in the club expected to see. Harriot was mine.
Michael was impressed. Even though the moment had become a weakened blip in her efforts of having me arrested, tortured and even killed, Harriot was in no way fighting off any of my advances, nor was she calling out for the officers around the edges of the dancefloor to come to her aid. As for Lady Dobrev, her silence waited to see what her friend's actions were going to be, whatever they were going to be. She was a great admirer of Harriot, she idolized her in a way that

decisions of any importance were left up to her, only then would she follow suit and ride it out, so to speak. And that night, she and Lady Sycamore were certainly riding out their differences.

The House Of Swan

From the nightclub, Michael and I had escorted the two ladies back to the apartment that I'd been frequenting the past few months. It was late on in the early hours before we all got down to sleep from the excitement throughout the day. This in mind, it was of no surprise when I awoke to find Harriot and Valerie both bludgeoned to death before me. The sight was quite sickening to my stomach, so much so that I could not refrain from throwing up several times while making my way to the bedroom door. Behind me were the women who had threatened me and Michael – Michael!
Rushing out of the bedroom and straight down the hallway into the living room, I scanned around quickly, before rushing even faster through another hallway and straight into Michael's bedroom without announcement. He wasn't there.
The healing wounds around my body began to pester me with their itching and sore irritation's, which burned into my skin with painful repercussions. The wound I had acquired on my chest was given to me by Dr. Lions, just before he met the end of a scalpel aimed at his head. It missed, unfortunately, clipping his neck and most probably severing a major artery, hopefully. The very thought of our ensuing fight was starting to bring me to a less stressed level, one which I could feel lifting of fear.

'Lucas, are you alright?' Michael shouted out at me when suddenly appearing from the bathroom door outside his bedroom. 'What's wrong?'
I couldn't believe he was even asking me!

'***You killed them!***' I gasped running up and grabbing him.
Michael's eyes showed nothing, no sorrow, no remorse, there was nothing at all to read from his expression except darkness.

'About that. You see, the funny thing is...'

'***WHY?***' I screamed out while tightening my grip of him.

'Because you're a Cavendish, and I'm a Gruber, so, if you look at it from that perspective, you'll find...!'

Before he could finish talking his shit I punched him clean in the face; his cheeks, nose and lips shuddered, bent, split and bled all at the same time. Michael gasped a low moan before his whole entire body fell to the ground in a heap, his arms, legs and head landing awkwardly between the bathroom door and hallway wall. I'd never hit anyone that hard before, not even Michael, as when I'd hit him before.

Looking down at his half-naked body covered only with a long white bath towel, I tried gathering my thoughts of what to do next – I was fluxed in the way of slight panic.

'Right now, I bet you're wondering if he's dead, or merely just unconscious!' The calm voice of Lady Ellington-Evermore sounded out to me from the apartments front door.

I didn't need to turn around to know who it was, or to whom the voice belonged, I already knew. But the strange appearance of my Cousin was baffling me more than the condition of my friend Michael laying still on the ground.

'You're risking a lot being here, Cousin,' I whispered.

'Not as much as you, I see. He isn't dead, however, so when you're ready we'll go!' She delivered an impossible assumption that gave warrant for an untimely response.

'***Go! Go where?***' I cried, breaking my stance and walking back through the apartment into the bedroom where there on the floor Melissa was repulsed by the spectacle of mutilation.

'***Oh My Fucking God!***' She managed to cry out before being violently sick down the hallway wall and onto the carpet.

I stood looking into the room at a sight which had been so pleasing to my eyes, the once white satin curtains closed to the sunlight that pierced the window and lit the walls up a dark crimson red. The body parts of the two women had been scattered aimlessly across the bedroom floor as if ripped apart and strewn in a fit of rage and madness. This was the work of a madman, no human could have done this through any other means than to be filled with pure bitter hatred of women.

'*Did you…!*'

I turned to Melissa as soon as she was able to speak again.

'What are you doing here, Melissa? Why are you hounding me like some lost love sick puppy running from its Master? You don't belong here…'

'Correct, but then neither do you, Lucas, The Hood is dead!'

I heard the bells of Borello chime, the sound was soothing to my ears, pleasant to my thoughts as my realization kicked in.

'You should know, Cousin, it was you and Lady Gruber who killed him. Now, cut the crap and tell me why you are really here? Are you alone? Are you armed?' I threw question after question at her, not once letting her answer the one, before she was answering another to a totally different query. Eventually I stopped, maybe it was to calm my guilt at seeing her face fall from a graceful smile, to something that resembled Lady Sycamore's severed head.

'If you come with me now, everything that you see around you will be cleaned up and put right. But you have to come now, Lucas, do you understand?'

This I understood. Even in Borello, my Cousin's hand reached as far as the same corrupt authorities as Lady Gruber. It would only be a matter of a single phone call to the Chief of Police and all the blood, guts and entrails from the murder scene would vanish into "It never happened".

'*Go fuck yourself!*' I shouted out at her. She was offended.

'You know I can make you return to Evermore, you stupid boy! The deal was that you stay…'

'*The deal!* You had me kidnapped, drugged, tortured…I died in that place, Melissa, don't you see? Everything that they say about that shithole is true…oh yeah, they experiment on their patients, make them do things…!' I broke down crying where I stood, to which Melissa attempted to console me by stepping forward, only for me to stop and look up at her coldly.

'Come back with me, Lucas, you'll be safe. I promise.'

And there it was, the statement that had sunk a thousand ships in the ocean of treachery and disaster both. Not that it was any way connected to me, but the deaths of the two women would have no reflection on Melissa either. Her request, be it later that of a demand that I accompany her back to Evermore, there was still that little question bouncing around in my head that begged to be answered. And only Lady Evermore could answer it.

'You came here alone, but why would you venture all the way from Evermore to…You were coming here to meet with someone, Michael! You were coming here to meet Michael, which means you and he are… ***Uh, that's not fucking right, Cousin!*** ' I put two and two together while connecting all of the dots and made a perfect five point zero on Melissa and Michael's sordid love affair.

'It's not what you think Lucas, my visit here was to see you and you alone. I have no idea where you get these ideas from, but be rest assured, as soon as you get home we'll get the doctor to see to your wounds…check your head, too!'

Melissa sounded sincere, she probably was, but I missed it from the moment she sat down on a chair resting against the hallway wall and whispered a name she didn't deserve the right to speak from her lips.

'Elizabeth was the only daughter of Mallandra's Sister, Susan, she used to run after baby Sheekan's and throw sticks at cats up in the trees, just to claim rewards from the owners. There were many special qualities about her, just none that I could ever condone as being good. You and her are so much alike, I doubt I'd know you apart if you were both the same sex!'

Melissa had actually made a joke, and it made me smile.

I had the unnerving feeling that I was somehow in the wrong place at the right time. Something was wrong; with the whole atmosphere of the building, of that room, of Melissa.

'Who is Alice Gruber, Cousin?' I asked with a look and tone that tore that smile from her face so quickly, and I'm so sure I heard the rip of skin as it fell.

Melissa stood and walked up to me, her eyes showing a need to speak, but for the sadness in her eyes she looked away. In all the time that I'd spent with her, never had I seen her this upset before. I believe she was herself crying silent tears.

'They will come for you...'

'Who will?' I demanded grabbing a hold of her shoulders and forcing her to turn and look at me. 'Who will come for me?'

Melissa hushed me with a gentle finger pressed over my lips.

'Shhh, listen to me. They will come for you both in the early hours. They won't kill you until you are put before them! I am so sorry that this couldn't have worked out better Lucas, but now you're on your own. If you stay here, then here will be the place you die. Come with me and we can stand together against Borello and win back our destiny's.'

A part of me wanted to believe Melissa, if only for the fact of her pre-warning me about The Resolve: Kill that which is most feared by the Bureaucracy and the ones taking a short fall.

'**Who is Lady Alice Gruber, Melissa?**' I demanded again, only this time I wanted – needed – to know the answer.

Shaking her head while shedding her tears she started to walk backwards toward the bedroom door, the pale silhouettes of armed response police officers making their final moves to be close enough to take a shot. Looking around me I saw the small window that looked down into the blackened Borello Black River, my belief that if I could make it to the window in time I could make my quick escape there and then, that way Michael would be safe and so would my evil Cousin, Melissa.

'Dark days are upon us all. I'll see you in hell!'

And with this said I ran into a sprint before diving up through the air into and through the window, it's hardened impact on my hands inflicting a sting as they smashed through the wooden glass panel's until finally I was feeling the sun on my body just before hitting the freezing cold waters below. The current was the hardest part of the most spectacular getaway, its power rolling and pulling me into its dark depths.

At the apartment Melissa rushed forward to look down into the murky depths of the river, and then turned away again before disappearing from the broken window completely.

'*You allowed him to escape!*' A man's voice exclaimed walking into the bedroom along with several armed officers.

'I wouldn't quite say that, not that it wasn't what I was trying to do, but more to the point you and your men were too close for a capture. Have your men check every house, door to door if you need to, and don't come back until I have an address or location of Lucas Cavendish.' Melissa roared out her orders to the man , a Lieutenant of The Borello Army.

'The Light will have your head for this, Lady Evermore, they do not tolerate failure as you Resheenian's openly except it to be a lesson, a sign, some magical corner stone that can be recut and retested for a better tomorrow. **YOU** have your forces on the Swift Bank closest to Evermore, concentrate of Verger, it's a twisty little fucker, but it will give you better ground if he has made it that far.'

'I will contact The House Of Swan immediately and have them send you more men for the…'

The Lieutenant put up a resisting hand. 'No, we cannot have them enter Borello, with The Lexicon Rule in place, it would break the truce both our towns have. Or is that your plan?'

Melissa was insulted. 'Have you been sniffing that gun oil again? Grow a pair and fuck off, and get someone to clear this mess up, too. Clean him up and get him back home to Alice, the less she fucking knows the better.'

It seemed strange to my Cousin that the Lieutenant left the apartment more worried than when he arrived, and this would have been because of the two Ladies lying dead on the floor in the bedroom. Still, she had to move on; either I was dead, or I was not dead, it was simple.

Unfortunately for me, my thoughts and impressions of the police there in Borello was to be my mistake; no sooner had I escaped through the window and made my way to the embankment on the other side of the river, than I was surrounded by my Cousin's Private Guard and frog marched back to the apartment where Melissa just stared at me.

'***Arrest him!***' The Lieutenant shouted as soon as he saw me.

'Cancel that order! Bring him here.' Melissa countermanded his order and had the Guards push me forward.

The Lieutenant was not happy with the declaration.

'He is to be…'
'He is to be taken back to Evermore…I assume that you were attempting to swim back home, Lucas?' She interrupted again, while turning to me with an expectant look.
I said nothing until the police left to exit the building.

The Ladies Of Valencia

Asking for a moment alone with Michael, Melissa gave a sighed "Okay" before telling me to meet her in the car outside as soon as I was done.
'You should go,' Michael whispered to me. 'Alice will know nothing of this…I promise.'
Leaving his side that day I returned to Evermore Manor with my Cousin, Melissa and her Personal Security Officer, Lyndon Frobisher. I did not like him – nor he me.
The drive from Borello to Evermore town took all of forty minutes, stopping off at Kirstie's Cakes for some underrated Golden Cupcakes. As nice as they were, however, Melissa had all of her priorities in the wrong order.
'***Cupcakes!***' I hissed angrily.
'They're for the Ball tonight. What's wrong, don't you like Cupcakes, Lucas?' She asked after revealing her plans for the evening. The Balls at Evermore were exclusive, glitzy and most of all, they were prestigious in the only way possible to any of the Rich Bloods who attended; Sorpium, Crientis, Harvegstar and Cornistori Ettel – The Gravelate Elustrielle.
I had been quite partial to the little cakes before The Institute, as well as many other delicious cakes and sweets, too, but at the moment my only concern was knowing "What was to happen now?"
Placing the large decorated cardboard box down between us on the back seat of the SLK, Melissa turned and looked at me.
'When I heard of your Cousin Xander O'Neill's death, I was completely inconsolable to the point of letting my heart break. It was his death that made me understand that there are a lot

of things out there today which can take us by surprise, even while we sleep. You have earned my Pardon, Lucas, you and your family. Tonight you will be the Host of The Evermore Grand Ball, and tonight, you will decide your own fate!'

I looked at her as though suspicious. '***My fate?***'

'You will have until Midnight tonight, to decide whether you are to stay with your family here in Evermore, or return to that god awful town, Borello. The choice is yours, of course.'

Melissa spoke calmly, precisely and with absolute sincerity. At first, as anyone would start to think, was the fact of whether she meant it, or if she was toying with me for some other reason known only to her?

'This Ball, is it…'

Melissa shushed me as she reached over and took a mobile phone from her purse to answer it. I sat silently listening and patiently counting the minutes until she finished the call, before continuing my questioning of The Ball.

'Is it important to you, Cousin?' I asked with a dead-look in my eyes that she responded to with equal tolerance.

'It is important to both of us, Lucas, can't you see that? You look for something in everyone, you always have, dear Cousin. You are so…' Melissa was fighting herself against the way she became transfixed for so long. '…I want you to know, however, you want to…***LUCAS!***'

My stare was broken by the loud screaming voice of Melissa inside the tight confines of the car, the brief start of panic and bolt of shock forcing me to move away from her. And, by the way in which she was looking at me now, you would have thought I'd grown horns on the top of my head.

'***Melissa!***' I responded. '***You're afraid!***'

There were not many things in Evermore, or perhaps all of Resheen, that my Cousin was afraid of, but for two things: Failure and Defeat. Simple "Failure" could be rebuilt, whereas "Defeat" was that one absolute action that would end her completely and without mercy.

'If you do the fucking Eye thing to me again, I will show you exactly who is afraid! You are way out of your depth here, I can tell you that for sure. Tonight, before Midnight, you make your decision. Do you understand?'

I nodded to the demonic lecture that convinced me that she was indeed being serious about my making a choice between the two towns, but I had no idea why she was doing this.

'Can I ask…'

'No. We're home now, so why don't you go on and follow Mr. Frobisher, he will show you to your room where you can clean up and get ready. I will have Doctor Philips call in and have you looked over before The Ball.' Melissa snapped before proceeding to tell me what I was to do, and who I was to see.

Mr. Frobisher was a man with the ability to take care of himself and those around him, which could only mean he was Ex-Gov: Military, Mercenary, Fixer, Mechanic – take your pick. Waving a hand for me to walk in front of him into the house, I smiled before copying his actions. He smiled back, nodded his head and lead the way into the large Bohemian Manor House.

'Soldier, right?' I blurted out looking around.

'Yes, nine years, Master Lucas,' Frobisher replied turning to face me as he continued walking through the hallways to the steep staircase leading up to the East Wing bedrooms.

'Did you see much action?' I asked casually.

Frobisher stopped at the foot of the staircase and turned to face me again, only this time he had a look in his eyes that in all my days, were the eyes of hell in sunder where only the ways of a trained man could possibly escape. Frobisher had seen death, and a good fair share of it, too.

'So, Master Lucas, what is it you are?'

The question was neither that, nor anything else for that matter. Was it a trick question?

'***Excuse me!***' I begged him to elaborate his query.

Lifting his shirt sleeve cuff up to his elbow he showed me a small tattoo, one which caused me to feel vulnerable, but at the same time happy for him. It was the insignia of The Black Flag Regiment, Task Force 101, Black Operations Indigo.

'***Captain David Price!***' I whispered a shocked gasp.

'You're Cousin, Lady Melissa, she only wants what is best for you, Lucas. Maybe we could socialize after The Ball, tomorrow evening, maybe?' Frobisher suggested.

If he wasn't sounding so crazy and letched by singing the praises of Lady Evermore, I'd have actually considered having a drink or two with him.

'My Cousin tried to kill me...'

'No, Doctor Lions tried to kill you, Lady Evermore believed you were taken with the...!'

I couldn't allow him to finish speaking the sentence, if I didn't want him dead, that was. He was talking of "The Evermore Curse", the bringer of madness, destruction and annihilation of all that is Evermore. It was unfounded.

'You think you know everything there is to know about me, don't you, Frobisher? I mean, you have that toy... **The Hive!** So, here's the deal, if you can tell me one thing that wasn't plucked from that rusty contraption in my Cousin's Study, I will get the first round of drinks in tomorrow evening myself.'

There was a slight pause that had me wondering whether he was considering the proposal, or simply calculating the odds of succeeding in the challenge. Either way, he was as wise as I saw him in that moment, clueless as to being intelligent enough to discover anything that I didn't already know.

'Your room is this way, Master Lucas, it's in the East Wing, so you don't have to worry about noises from our unsettled guests!' He laughed out suddenly before returning back to a normal civilized tone. 'I trust this evening will be both exciting and insightful for the both of us, I'm sure you will agree. If you need anything, ring One on your dialing pad, but be aware, I don't fetch anything that I wouldn't fetch myself. Here we are.' Opening the door to the bedroom I looked inside briefly and then with an about face, I turned to Frobisher.

'Can I ask whose on the guest list for The Ball tonight, Mr. Frobisher? You never know, there may be someone on there that is a threat or...'

'The Guest List is vetted vigorously, Master Lucas, so if there are any persons who are a threat to Evermore, we will be on it like a bug to a windshield.'

Again, I asked, just to make sure that his response was the same as before, only this time offering my own services.
He nodded his head from side to side. 'I'm afraid not, Master Lucas, that information is Privy to your Cousin and Chief of Security. There is one thing that I can tell you about this big shindig, and that's what is on the food menu.' He laughed as if in his own mind he thought it a funny joke.
As difficult as I found it to shrug the whole thing off, I was now curious to the question I was asking myself: Could I take him? He was a strapping thirty-something ex-Special Forces soldier, most probably trained in the deadly arts of hand-to-hand combat and all the other bullshit that came along with it.

'If you could get me a copy of the menu that would be great, Frobisher, if it isn't too much trouble that is?' I said with a semi-conscious low tone that hid the sarcasm much too well.
His train of thought was derailed – badly.

'I...erm! Well, I can certainly do that for you, Master Lucas, no rules broken in that, I hope!' He replied with caution.
Informing me to be ready by seven-thirty, he left me to sort myself out. The bedroom was dim and smelling of wood polish that stayed fresh in the air, the curtains were thick but drawn half way, while the sunlight from the day outside was fighting to get inside and brighten up the room.

A Shade Of Red

The run of Borello partying had caught up with me with an unrelenting vengeance that had me rest for the whole entire day, the welcome of sleep in a comfortable bed that put me out into the Land of Nod, until eventually I awoke to the sound of the House Staff changing shifts. It was 6.00pm.
Cleaning myself up with a shower and quick shave, I dressed into the clothes left out on the bed for me to wear for The Ball; the dark black Rahun suit jacket, the trousers mid-tied and even a white Beracci shirt and black Crown shoes to match. It felt comfortable, but it didn't quite feel like me when looking

at myself in the mirror.

A knock at the door brought an elderly man I had never seen at the Manor before, Richard, the replacement of some other Staff Hand who had died suddenly in his sleep a few months ago, but again, another Staff Hand I didn't know.

'Your mask, Master Lucas, for tonight's Masquerade Ball.'

I took a small oblong box from him with a slight nod as confirmation, before he left and closed the door behind him to return downstairs.

Standing in front of the mirror I opened the box and took from it a Bon Efitite in neon blue, the center piece of the mask itself blackened with a dark satin finish that highlighted the holes to the eyes. This was definitely me. The adjusting of the facial garment gave me an idea, one that would give me a head start, so to speak, on all those pursuers who came to chase me down in Borello. It was the afterthought that hit me hard; my fate still hung in the balance with my Cousin, so what if I was to choose Evermore over Borello? What if I was to choose Borello over Evermore and become impossibly faced with undefeatable odds?

Making my way out of the room I was stopped by Frobisher, who in his wisdom decided to take away the security detail for the event from the upper two floors of the Manor, something that would be frowned upon by Melissa.

'Are we expecting uninvited guests, Frobisher?' I asked with a raised smile that seemed to threaten him in some way.

He informed me of my role of being Lady Evermore's Consort for the evening ahead, while this was already cleared by Melissa herself, and that it would be better to focus the strengths of the security detail to the main parts of the building. Of course, me being me, I put into question the fact that the upper floors of the Manor were the most vulnerable, like the roof for instance.

'My Cousin, where is she now?'

Frobisher pointed down from the balcony to a small door at the left of the stairs in the lower hallway. 'In there, but I wouldn't disturb her, she's with guests, Master Lucas.'

It was fine, I had no real intentions of seeing her anyway; the shorter the evening to drive the time to Midnight the better.

'Some things will never change!' I said before descending the stairs and making my way into The Great Hall of Luxton; the original families name of Borello and all that it contained within its large town. The mere presence of something so symbolic as to associate Borello with Evermore was Historic to some, while insulting to others. Here I was met by Quimby Jones, an American big shot from New York, and his friend, Jerimiah O'Donnell of Dublin, Ireland. The two gentlemen, though wearing a mask, didn't seem that shy or bothered by revealing their true identities to anyone, especially me.

'Quite a big turnout this time,' Quimby gloated around the room at all the well-dressed ladies that passed him by. 'I have no idea what this big surprise is of Lady Evermore's, however, they say it is of a surprise that will enlighten us to the true meaning of our endeavor's.'

Jerimiah was set back in his attitude, less his childish youth filled face that had become weathered by the trips abroad over the past several decades. Though he said very little, it was Quimby who made up for the loss.

'The Ball is for everyone, isn't it, Gentlemen?' I put forward to them both. With a weak nod Quimby clammed up.

'This is your first time in Evermore, I take it?' Jerimiah sighed.

I nodded. 'First time in a long time. I hear the Lady of The Manor has a surprise for someone this evening, is this true?'

I was baiting the two men, to find out a little more of what they knew, but even they didn't know anything that Melissa didn't want them to know.

'Whatever plans Lady Melissa Evermore has made for the evening, you can be rest assured that it will be something so wonderful and magical, I just know we will all be impressed.'

Quimby cried out to the loud objectable shushes from several people standing around us.

'Maybe they have something to do with Lady Evermore's god awful pathetic Cousin, Master Lucas?' I whispered a seed that the two gentlemen responded to unexpectedly.

Quimby, his whole posture, laughable 'Feel Good' smile and attention leer at a very voluptuous young woman dancing in front of him grinded to an absolute halt; the eyes squinting on my mask covered face, while the gasping up of the right words to say choked his exhaling breath.

'***Master Lucas!*** You offend his name and me, Sir, whoever you are?' Quimby eventually managed to cry out.

It was a sudden thought that maybe Quimby was one of the Fan Club followers of my previous 'Moonlighting' in Borello, though his appearance and manner did not fit the profile I had built up in my mind of him.

'Isn't that the fellow who Melissa took in and helped when his house burnt down to the ground?' Jerimiah blurted, his memory of my Family Home being destroyed coming to mind. Quimby nodded his head vigorously. 'Yes, that's right. Lucas is a man who I believe can change the whole situation around in our favor, my dear friend. I am not one to talk out of class, but I hear that his recent stint across the America's has brought him to a place of peace. It has to be trust and admiration only, I'm afraid, his time during the Fifty Day War was so tragically misleading, I'm sure you will agree, Jerimiah?'

I couldn't believe what I was hearing from the two gentlemen, here I was standing before them with only a mask to hide my one true identity – a Masquerade Mask at that. I had been mind fucked! Now I had no other alternative than to find out more.

'Gentlemen, I have an appointment with a Lucky Lady.' I politely excused myself from their presence.

Quimby gave out a loud belly laugh that had almost half the people in the hall looking over at us, Quimby over-joyous, Jerimiah in a state of Flux and me, having the look of dread written all over my face.

'And who is this Lucky Lady, my dear boy?'

'That my friend, is up to the Lady,' I replied walking away through the crowded gathering in the direction of the small door where my Cousin was still entertaining her VIP Guests. My hand reaching out for the handle, it was grabbed by a firm hand on my shoulder. It was Frobisher.

'I did inform you that Lady Evermore is in a Private Meeting, Master Lucas!' He whispered coldly. 'If you'd like, I can show you through to the conservatory, your friend is waiting for you there and wishes a private audience!'

If there was anything that annoyed me more than Authority and its corrupt processing of having a single thought invest in the rise to self-conceited wealth, it was the disadvantage of others that cradled the belief they knew more than yourself.

'***My friend, Frobisher!***' I exclaimed grabbing a glass of champagne from the passing waiter's tray.

'A Mr. Connor Derby, from Redstone, Master Lucas. He says he is in an urgent need of a chat, so I took the liberty of showing him into the conservatory so you could speak without any interruptions. I have sent some drinks and food through. Would you like me to inform Lady Evermore?'

I wasn't used to this kind of nicety, to be completely honest, it was starting to make me feel uneasy.

'No, it's alright, I will go and see Mr. Derby, you don't have to worry my Cousin with this, are we clear Frobisher?' I warned in a way that he could understand my wishes.

He nodded. 'Very well, I will go and tend the Main Entrance until the event begins.'

His agreeing look gave me confidence, both of knowing he would keep my friends arrival between the three of us and, that of a mental and physical build to my own self being.

Leaving Frobisher I made my way through the last of the large crowd blocking the hall's entrance, before taking a little short cut I knew of via the kitchens and work house at the rear of the Manor. Once clear of the short fence that came to circle around the rear entrance into the conservatory, I was finally facing a young man dressed in casual clothing; leather jacket, jeans, t-shirt and trainers. In his hand he held a thin blue file.

'***Lucas!*** Is that you?' He asked with uncertainty.

I didn't answer straight away, due to the fact that the young man standing there in the room was reported to have been killed in a motoring accident. He didn't look dead to me!

'***Connor Derby!***' I exclaimed suddenly walking closer to him. '***Welcome back from the grave!***'

It was something of a shock seeing Connor standing there as if he had never left Evermore to race, but that was a whole other story entirely, he was alive and that was all that mattered.

'We heard about your quick trip to The Institute, how did it go?' He asked jokingly but also cautiously.

Connor was my friend once upon a time, as kids we did everything that the others didn't want or need to do. The day that I was to be drugged and bundled into the back of a white van and taken against my will to The Saunders' Institute, Connor was on his way back to Evermore to pick me up. His return to Redstone for all the wrong reasons were to be our "Regrets", while it was later I heard of his tragic loss, one that I understood completely at the heavy cross that he was baring on his shoulders.

'Not turning into a Mangina now, are you Connor?' I gave a forced smile that forced a short laugh. With this Connor moved in closer and gave me a man-hug before laughing out himself.

It was good to see him again, alive, too, which was a bloody great bonus for us both.

'***The Jackal?***' I whispered.

He nodded his head silently.

'No matter, next time, perhaps!' I rose my glass of champagne up and saluted him with a graceful nod.

It was then that I saw the look in his face.

'I have to ask, Lucas, what we are doing...'

'***Natasha!*** It had to be Natasha!' I exclaimed placing the glass down on a nearby cabinet and patting Connor on the side of his arm in a friendly way before walking over to the drinks and food that Frobisher had put out for us. 'Do you love her?'

'I think so...I mean, yes, I do, she and her Father...!'

'I see!' I became angry at the fact that it was our arrangement, whether it was with honor or agreement of any other reward, that he had sworn his life on carrying out a simple plan.

'Exactly how close are you, Connor?'

His break in composure brought a few questions, whilst the

main question was that of his loyalty, and whether it still remained as founded as we had left it five years ago.

Connor found himself a seat and sat down before telling me in great detail of the way things went in Redstone, everything that I needed to know to assess our options. The way I saw it by the end of the tale, Connor was 'Out'. He wanted to take the chance and opportunity to get the hell out of The Game.

'My Cousin will not be so forgiving, Connor. I was hoping…'

'I thought that you were…Oh, right, sorry!'

The cryptic interruption was of no help to my wondering what the hell he was talking about in suggesting wanting out.

'Thought what, Connor? Listen, you go and do what you want to do – what you need to do. I have some business here at Evermore before I can start worrying about Redstone, that place is far from being important…'

'**Somersby, he's alive!**' Connor revealed with a sustained voice that was filled with regret, rather than relief. 'He ran me off the road on my return here, I've been running ever since. We have a place up north, which is why, as soon as I heard you were back, I would come and see you.'

Nodding my head I turned and walked back the way I came to the conservatory, pausing at the doors while looking over my shoulder at a perturbed Connor Derby.

'Natasha! You and her have my blessing, but you know what this means? Good luck, Connor, you will have your reward by dawn tomorrow.'

A confirming smile ended our meeting on a high note, at least.

Passion Before Midnight

I had made my way back into the Manor, while all around me were multitudes of truly astonishing bearers of dress; the reds, blues, flame burnt oranges and pastel greens. All shading's of dresses, bodices and even provocatively bare essential costumes walked, floated and even glided past my eyes in a show of flavor and grace.

'Don't you just love these get together's?' The sudden sound of Melissa whispered unexpectedly from behind me.

Turning to face her I showed no emotional response to her presence or answer to her question. This annoyed her greatly.

'Who are all these people, Melissa?' I asked with an immediate demand from her to keep my voice down as not to reveal her true identity to everyone.

'Names, Lucas, are not needed here, not tonight. Why don't you go and mingle with the guests and return here before Midnight, so as not to put a dampener of things for you making your decision. I hear Jerimiah and Quimby have been their usual selves!'

The moment wasn't spoilt by the hinted reminder that I was there at Evermore Manor for a reason and one reason only, and, for the fact that no matter what my dear Cousin did to me, it's delivery of punishment would be heavenly compared to that of The Institute.

'You say that as if you are hiding from someone! Maybe you should practice what you...!'

The most warming sensation filled my cheek in a second of stinging pain that my senses absorbed with a fixing smile. She had slapped me – hard!

'Watch your fucking mouth, Cousin! We all have crosses to bare and some soul sucking predator wanting to find us, so you be a little more respectful. Midnight, you have three hours. Now, fuck off and stop cramping my style!' She warned me with a finishing smile that stirred my fond memories of her.

We were younger, Melissa 15 and I only 12, when both of our parents were lost to the Madness Curse! Apparently. Melissa was a completely different person back then, she was more compassionate and caring than any of the other docile family members of The Evermore's, though it never silenced the way my family were constantly reminded of their place – which was neither here nor there, as regards to "Blood". My Father, however, had paid his dues, supported and fought for The Evermore's in every turn of events that threatened their existence – in return he was shunned.

'What will happen when there are no more Evermore's, Melissa?' I remember asking her on the day that her Aunt Rachel Barrisa-Evermore came to take her away to safety – away from me.

'Then it will be you, my Dear Cousin, who takes the throne!' She laughed into a passing vapor of my childhood memory, as from behind me a woman tapped gently on my shoulder.

'Hello, I'm Elizabeth, would you like to dance?' She asked in a well-orchestrated fashion that warned me that she was possibly on hire from Melissa. The name of the woman was one of the first warnings, while the second, that of the woman's flesh – her misplaced setting of that cheap Slanguage and cleanliness.

'Elizabeth, what a lovely name. I'm afraid I don't dance, I have two very stubborn left feet. Maybe we could...'

'**Fuck!**' She exclaimed nervously.

'Or we could do that, I guess!' I returned the answer with raised eyebrows at the directness of the woman.

Taking her by the arm gently, I led her through the house until finally stopping outside my room upstairs in the East Wing. At first we kissed, but then Elizabeth, whom I doubted was her real name, began to unbutton my shirt very quickly.

'You have such a fine body, Master Lucas...I mean, Oh, fuck it!' She hesitated her mistake before unleashing the beast inside her like it was feeding time at the zoo; my shirt was gone, not ripped but taken and strewn onto the floor, as were those of my trousers which were flung over the closet door.

Suddenly she stopped, it was hardly a short pause, but an action that brought her to look down at me.

'Why don't you carry on and finish what my Cousin paid you to do, and if you're lucky, we will have sex before I go and find said Cousin, and tear her heart out of her chest!' I sneered as she finally removed the tight fit Boxer Shorts which hid the throbbing hardness that she grabbed a hold of straight away to take into her mouth. With a resisting hand I stopped her, pushing her determined head away from me gently. The woman became frustrated.

'Do I not please you, Master Lucas?' She asked confused.

It was something of a pleasure that I wasn't used to – had never gotten used to – in all my time at Evermore Manor; it was through the perkules of Status and Position that many of those previous Overseers to the House became righted with the finer things that included favor and entitlement. Go back two centuries and what you had were the Courtesan's, their services unlimited to Master and Lord, unlike today. And then you had the likes of Lady Melissa Evermore, crying down the lines of family elsewhere around the world claiming that of being bankrupt, while she hosted excessive expensive parties, functions and conducting Meet and Greets with investors as though she was the last of the big spenders. Which one was true, I had no idea.

'What's your name?' I asked her lighting up a cigarette I'd taken from my shirt pocket. **'You're real name!** '

Knelt down in front of me with both her breasts hanging out of a dirty bra that had been worn for some time without being changed, the woman bowed her head and fell into a silence that I knew only too well.

Sat smoking my cigarette until there was just but a quarter left on the tip, I stubbed it out in the circular chromed ashtray at the side of me. Again, I asked her what her name was?

'Angela,' she replied finally.

My gaze into her face was not a happy one, as she could well see and notice by my removing her hand from my genitals and standing to my feet. I was all but naked except for my socks.

Walking around her I lowered a hand to brush my fingers over the tops of her shoulders – she shuddered excitedly.

'Do you know who I am, Angela?'

'My Master for the evening!' She replied with slight doubt.

I laughed out loudly bending down to take a firm hold of her elbow before pulling her up onto her feet to face me.

'You are that of a gift…from my Cousin, Lady Evermore!' I whispered softly, looking her deep in the eyes.

Angela said nothing, she nodded once before returning her gaze to the floor, as if she half expected me to tell her to leave

my company and return to The Ball. But I wasn't about to do that, not to her. I remembered a time so long ago, the same scenario, but different surroundings. The Archaos of Societal wounds passed on the House Rules: No Fraternizing With The Staff. But, of course, it was "Love" that was a victim under the very same faction and rule.
Evermore House had its own history of seedy involvements with the Staff Hands, quite a few over the generations who went on to become the illegitimate Father's to the Bastard Children of "The Rich Bloods" and alas, victims to their desires and orders from other well respected Lords, Ladies and Gentlemen. It truly existed within the hidden bureaucracy.

'I serve you freely, Master Lucas,' she whispered moving her head forward toward me. 'You are safe.'
Angela's eyes burnt with both passion and loathing, of what it was that she had a hang up about, I didn't really want to know. Nodding my head from side to side I turned away and sought out my clothing and putting them back on gradually. Angela was suddenly afraid.

'Please…don't do this, Master Lucas!' She cried out rushing up behind me and throwing two tight arms around my waist. 'If we do not make love, Lady Evermore will be so cross. We could both be punished!'
The thought of something strange going on around the house was not far from the truth, Melissa had already set me up with a cheap virgin Whore, though also a Staff Hand, I very much doubted that this woman had ever been with another man – ever. Unfortunate was the case of my Relationship Status, if that is what you would refer to my involvement with the female Assassin of Borello, Lady Elizabeth Spink's.

'It's fine, just tell her we fucked, and I will fill in all the blanks for her pleasure and approval. Tell me, did you think we were going to be coming back to my room and doing anything but talking?' I advised her what to say to any enquirer's, and yet, the after thought was a little pre-designated.

'I was told you like the name Elizabeth, and that I would have the opportunity to lose my innocence to you, Master Lucas. I

was told you have not had a woman for a long time.'
The whole set-up started to make perfect sense, and even the whole organizing of The Ball, too, which had been called in my favor of Melissa's new plan. The only problem I had now, was that Midnight was only one hour and eighteen minutes away.

'Another town, another city, another life, Angela. Let me take a look at you...'

'*Why?*' She yelped as soon as I reached a hand out for her.

'So that I know which parts to eat and which parts to throw away!' I answered the not so intelligent question.
Angela was not stupid, or slow, or even uneducated.

'I think...I think you're very rude, Master Lucas. Rude and obnoxious...and if I could...'
Pulling Angela toward me we kissed; her voice silenced, her lips puckered, she was warming to the feeling that right now she could not focus on anything but the kiss. I let her go after just a minutes of forcing her lips to open wider with mine, our tongues deep throating one another until finally retracting to end our embrace.

'You taste like strawberries!' I said, suddenly looking away from the young woman. 'You taste of strawberries and warm hazelnut vanilla. I guess the real question wasn't asking you what your name is, but rather, who the hell do you work for?'
Angela stood with a vacant stare. 'I am nobody.'
I very much doubted that she was nobody, especially how only two people knew of a finer detail that Elizabeth had, and that was herself and me. The Strawberries and soft warm hazelnut vanilla taste, that was something that both me and Elizabeth always sought out around the town. Of course, there was only two places in the whole of Resheen where you could get the favorite ice cream dish, one of those places being The Bastion Tavern, in Borello.

'I'm sorry, I didn't mean to...*I'm sorry!*'
I grabbed a hold of her gently but firmly to pull her back to me without making her trip or fall in the process.

'Did my Cousin send you to get information out of me?'
Angela nodded truthfully. 'No.'

If Melissa had not sent Angela to get something that she could use against me at a later date, then what was the purpose of her being here with me this night? No matter how much I thought about the whole thing, I couldn't convince myself to accept the possible truth – that Angela was a Pawn, and she didn't even know it. The thought that she had been inserted within the House by some other means did trigger – but which one?

'Tell me something about yourself, Angela, it's alright, you don't have to tell me anything you don't want to.' I reassured her to the fact that she would eventually tell me everything.

For the remainder of the time I had before the starting of the big event, both Angela and I sat talking about her family; sisters, brothers, aunts and uncles, who were back home in Borello. And for such a young woman she had all the hallmarks of someone who would work for my Cousin, maybe even that of an Assassin Guild!

'So, you were asked to seduce me by Melissa, and then you...' Angela laughed into her hand. '***Seduce!*** I'm sorry, but if there is any seducing going on here, Master Lucas, it certainly isn't from me!'

Maybe it was true, maybe the seduction point of my concern was that of a growing paranoia forcing me to believe she was something other than a Spook! Maybe, if I rested the heavy questioning for a while, she may have the chance to prove herself.

'***You look tense!***' Angela spoke up an observation pressing her hands into my shoulders gently. 'Maybe you need to lie down for a little while?'

I didn't question or argue the suggestion, which happened to be a good idea, though revealing this fact was clear on my face. Lying down on top of the bed with outstretched arms reaching up to the trestle head board, I laid my head onto the pillow as Angela climbed up onto the bed and over to straddle my waist. With a soft needing and rubbing motion applied to my scarred shoulder blades and healing back, she began to sing a song – to herself, I thought at first.

'That's a nice song, Angela, where did you learn that?' I asked between groans of pleasurable rubs that began to make their way into the center of my spine – a place nobody touched. I didn't resist to her further massaging.

'Everyone learns it in Borello, Master Lucas, even the unborn babies,' she whispered. 'Would you like me to teach it to you?'
The offer was tempting, though I never had the voice chords for singing to anyone but myself, and even then, that was rare.

'No, it's Okay, I'm from Evermore, we don't sing songs that are from Borello.' I sighed deeply before I tried to concentrate on the excruciatingly pleasurable sensation filling my entire body as Angela slid both thumbs all the way down my spine. It tingled twice before I gave my first raised reaction, and then the second that arched my upper torso and brought me to turn over onto my back to face her bewildered stare.

'How old are you, Angela, if you don't mind me asking?'
She told me she was nineteen, twenty in a few weeks, though she looked younger because when she was a girl, she caught Scarlet Fever. I guess it would have been very uncomfortable her having such a nasty condition at such a young age.
Proceeding to massage my back her hands made their way up to the tops of my shoulders and squeezed into the muscle.

'Will you be returning to Borello, Lucas, I mean, will you choose Borello?' She asked to my surprise.
I didn't answer. I couldn't answer, for the fact that she was no person that I knew, or trusted. Instead I flipped over onto my back and took a firm hold of her wrists and pulled her toward me quickly, before stopping her within inches of my face. In that solitary, silent unknown moment I lifted my head from the pillow and gave her a look that had her bend down and kiss my lips with a slow, passionate need. It was effortless, though not without its complications with the short time I had left before having to return to Melissa, but Angela led the way; her gyrating hips making my crouch stir, her hands which I had now let go made their way around my neck, wrapping around me to give her enough leverage to mount my now throbbing hard cock and sink down onto its long, wide girthed shaft.

'*Christ!*' She moaned, releasing her hold of my neck and

pushing herself up until she was sitting upright. I stopped her.
  '***Wait!***' I called out softly.
Repositioning myself underneath her, I used my hands to lift her up slightly from my hardness, and then lowered her down again while pushing myself up into her tight depths.
  'Better?' I smiled.
Angela smiled back at me with a pleasurable gasp. 'Better.'
We made love like two complete strangers meeting for the very first time, our hearts rested, our commitment unneeded, as we lived in the feeling, the emotion and the free spirited call of an Animalistic rage. Leaving us both invigorated, zesty and out of breath we both collapsed and laid side by side of one another. By the time the knock came to the door we had already dressed and readied ourselves. Frobisher looked surprised by the way in which Angela and I walked from my room, a form of half-envy at seeing the young woman who followed out after me.

Death Is Only The Beginning

The Main Hall was quiet, but certainly not empty by the time the three of us reached the doors. Seeing everyone in their masks lining themselves up against all four walls, while Melissa and another woman beckoned us up to the front of the Hall where two chairs had been prepared for us to sit.
  'What the hell is this Frobisher?' I whispered a demanding cry at my Cousin's PA.
  'With respect, Master Lucas, I would really advise you to go with this, it is your moment.' He replied passing by me and making his way up to Melissa.
The Masquerade Ball was not as advertised to me by Melissa, it was a ceremony, one of those bare breasted, pop-socked, up your bollocks kind that Captain David Price had warned me about several years ago.
Finally reaching the plinth that stood four feet from the floor, I was shown to my seat and given a small envelope, as was Angela, too. The contents unknown, I was sure that soon I

would find out what they were.

Standing forward of us Melissa raised her hands and asked for silence from all the guests, who immediately obliged.

'My Cousin, Lucas, has for many years now been loyal to his family here in Evermore. He has faced nothing less than his fair share of challenges, pain and loss...' Melissa began with a sham speech. '...even of love! It was five years ago, that Lucas began his long journey to America...'

The charade was insulting. '***Stop!***'

As soon as I yelled out I was grabbed by the hand, by one of Melissa's personal guards – or so I thought at first – which had me readying myself to turn and lash out, until I caught sight of a woman's hand – Angela.

'**Lucas!** How much have you drank tonight?' Melissa attempted to pass the incident off with a joke of intoxicated behavior. This did not work, however, for the fact that a low whistle melody was given from the crowd – familiar!

Looking down at Angela expecting to see her whistling the song that she was singing back in the bedroom, I saw only the look of fear on her face. I gave her a strained smile.

'Relax, you'll be Okay, trust me!' I whispered down to her as I returned my searching gaze of the crowd for the source to the tune being whistled. Melissa, too, now looked around, as did several others who were curious. Frobisher left my side to take his place next to Melissa to protect her.

'My heart belongs to that dashing fellow, the one who found me in Borello,' the whistler now changed to singing the lyrics of the tune. It was a female voice – a woman. 'His Masterate I would Masturbate forevermore, if that young fellow really was from Evermore.'

The woman stepped out of the clearing crowd to reveal herself to both Melissa and me, something that had an instant spark of panic and an atmosphere so highly strung that I could sense, feel and taste the bloody violence well before all hell was to be set loose.

'***Deadly Night Shade!***' Angela gasped, catching sight of Elizabeth at the very same time as I did.

Melissa ordered her Private Guards to seize Elizabeth, at first, before seconds after giving them permission to shoot her where she stood. For Elizabeth she didn't seem to be worried one bit, while my Cousin and the roomful of guests stood in anticipation of the guns sounding off their loud rounds.

'*You think you can kill me with bullets!* ' Elizabeth shouted out with raised hands with Erulium bracelets that the bullets ricocheted off of as if they were of no immediate danger or threat to her.

Realizing that Elizabeth was right, Melissa raised a single hand in the air and ordered her guards to stop firing. When the last gun had silenced, it was then the turn of a different method – archers with the precision to stun, wound and even kill any living thing within one hundred and thirty yards.

Elizabeth now looked worried. 'I have come for you, Melissa Ellington-Evermore…to take you to hell!'

Odd was the fact that when people ran their mouths off to others who were less confident and strong, it would end with the show of force, sometimes with a passionate show of rage – and Melissa certainly had this going on inside her.

'*STOP!* Everyone stop what you are doing and stand very still. Right now, we can talk this through, I'm sure. Elizabeth, I want you to surrender…if you don't…'

Elizabeth made her way forward and bowed down to my Cousin, her eyes to the ground, a concealed hand perched lightly around her long broadsword. Frobisher attempted to intervene and warn Melissa of the risk, but she shooed him away from her side with a waving hand.

'Forgive me for being so late, Lady Evermore, as you will see, I have killed all but a few of your Private Army! Do you wish me to continue?'

For a moment I thought that Elizabeth was going to surrender herself, as did all the attending guests who turned around to look at one another and whisper under quiet breath. It was only when I saw the glint of the blade hit the moonlight, that from my mind's eye I began to re-enact that of Elizabeth's Mother being murdered in Borello. The memory was painful, so much so that I could not stand the torturous vision – I gave out a loud agonizing scream before falling into the darkened veil of unconsciousness: in the fading moment of losing consciousness I saw the blade slicing through the air, through the soft and tender skin of my Cousin's neck. It's sharpened edge finding no difficulty in carrying its weight through and out the other side, as with a glazed look in Melissa's eyes, her head fell from her shoulders and fell to the floor. Melissa was dead!

The Prodigal Son Of Borello

The unconscious state that I was in brought a luring darkness that for me felt soothing, almost Majestic in its warmth and the heightened sensation of rising. And after several hours of being watched over and cared for, I finally opened up my eyes to a deeply saddened familiar face.

'Lord Lucas, you're awake at last!' Frobisher was suddenly pleased to see me alive, but rather than put pressure on those of my family and friends, he kept the least possible outcome to himself. 'Welcome back from the grave!'
One thing that I could never understand about Resheen, was the way in which you were greeted after losing any kind of physical consciousness. Maybe this was some kind of Frobisher thing, but then I remembered another saying it to me – Michael.

'***Where's my Cousin?***' I demanded, standing to my feet to find nausea and its reinforcements ambushing me into a very quick submission of restraint.
I didn't black out, but I felt that I was very close to it. In the very instance that I started to look feint, it was Frobisher who began talking me through the antidote to counter act its effect.

'***Breathe!*** Breathe slowly…slower, that's it. Three…look at me, two, you're doing fine, one.!'
I was out of it, snapped by a quick shake of my head and aware of my surroundings instantly. My one thought at that time was

why I didn't collapse back into unconsciousness, when clearly I was light headed enough to put at least three young men the same age, weight and size as me on their arses!

'How did you…never mind! Where is my Cousin?' I asked him again, only this time with a little more aggression in my tone of voice.

He told me that she was dead, first as last, and then went on to tell me that Elizabeth was loose. Initially I was deeply saddened by the tragic news of my Cousin's death, and yet, I was filled with joy deep down inside that Elizabeth was still alive. Of course, it was Title that stood tradition, and for this they needed a successor – me!

'What are your orders, Sir?' Frobisher asked.

I was now in a state of Flux: This was not good.

'Bring in the Reserve Army from the East of Evermore and two units from the North Side Wastelands. Bring me The Borello vigilante Deadly Night Shade – **Alive!**' I ordered him to bring in the necessary reinforcements in which to fortify Evermore against any further surprise attacks, while putting aside my emotions of Elizabeth. My orders were Protocol, not the start of a Witch Hunt that would end with more casualties.

'**Alive, Sir!**' Frobisher dared to question me. I gave a look so cold that it had him turn away from me with a twitch. 'Yes, Lord Lucas, she is to be taken alive. Understood.'

Leaving me to get my bearings I walked over to the window and looked outside, the sun was rising over The Crest of Evermore, over near the Old Mill and The Briary. It looked absolutely magnificent with the huge ball of yellow fire, it's immaculate reaching rays that illuminated the nearby clouds and finally set off the Majestic skyward patterns that if watched long enough, brought inner peace to one's soul.

'**She will be the death of you, Brother!**' Michael's voice cut across the room. He was standing near the door, one hand in his pocket while holding a cigarette in the other.

Turning to face him I gave a short risen smile of seeing him again, before forcing myself to lose it and approach him.

'How did you get past the Guards, Michael?' I asked puzzled.

Michael was being passive, blowing the smoke from his lungs out of his mouth toward me, while breaking his composure and standing up straight.

'Actually, Lucas, the question you should be asking is, how did Elizabeth Spinks escape a secure holding of Evermore? I mean, is the security normally this sloppy?' He joked.

His statement brought a thought to the forefront of my mind, the actual words of "Security" and "Sloppy", especially.

'*Lockdown!*' I exclaimed before quickly ushering him into the room and closing the door behind us. 'You know what a Lockdown is, don't you Michael?'

His blank but perturbed expression seemed to give it away that he obviously did know what a Lockdown was, as well as knowing exactly what could happen to him after the whole Manor House was secured by the Personal Guards.

'Do you know what I feel like right now?' He cried clasping his hands together and rubbing them gleefully.

I couldn't help but notice how relaxed and calm he was.

'Like a fucking rat in a maze, I should imagine!' I joked dryly.

Michael laughed. 'Close, but not quite. I feel like a drink...do you want one?'

Walking over to the mini-bar he prepared us a drink each before holding his up in the air. 'To good friends, may our friendship grow beyond brotherhood.'

His words were almost fateful, because as soon as he had said them and we raised our glasses together, the door of the room crashed open to the loud screams of Frobisher's voice filling the air to arrest Michael. His actions allowed by myself and the man that they were besieging, while manhandling and punching him in the chest and stomach. This was a manner in which I was only too happy to cease immediately.

'*Release him!*' I shouted out walking up to Michael.

Frobisher was hesitant, maybe too hesitant for my liking.

'***But he is the enemy, Sir!***'

Over the past decades of growing up at Cavendish House and here at Evermore Manor, it seemed to be the constant want and need to introduce hatred of our neighbors into all of our

family ways – The Ellington-Evermore Way. This was not my way, as both Frobisher and Michael Slattery were to discover.
I called one of the armed Private Guards to me and ordered him to hand over his side arm pistol.
'Enemy, Mr. Frobisher, what exactly do you mean by that?'
My question was disorientated in its delivery, as without as much as a wayward glance away from the weapon, we all began to notice Mr. Frobisher break his stance.
'My humble apologies, Sir, but I thought that...!'
I did not hesitate in putting him in his place right there in front of the Guards and Michael.
'Michael Slattery is my honored guest, Mr. Frobisher, and as so, I would remind you that guests of this house are to be respected by all Staff and at all times. Now, tell me, who is Michael Slattery?'
Frobisher was embarrassed, humiliated even, by the torment of my anger and rage at his outburst. Finally he nodded slowly.
'Michael Slattery is your guest, Sir, excuse the intrusion.'
And with this Frobisher led the Private Guards from the room and on to search the rest of the Manor. I returned the Guards weapon to him with a nod, before he rushed to catch up with Frobisher and the others.
Michael was quiet. Too quiet.
'While in The Institute, I met a man called Blackwell, a local family man whose only vice was to make one bet per week on The Borello Town Sweepstakes. His daughter, Megan, she was taken to The Borello Orphanage, where she stayed for two years before dying of pneumonia at age nine. Blackwell was a man of honor and great courage, his ridicule of torture brought him to one outstanding truth – he was going to die in that messed up madman's clinic. The last time I saw him was when the psychotic Doctor Lions transferred me to an alternate wing of the Institute, one where nobody could hear the patients scream...and scream they did, my friend. Blackwell told me of an organization in Borello, one which I have only heard the name of once...'
Michael butted in with a sigh. '***The Circle!***'

He was right, and unbeknown to me, it was "The Circle" that Michael himself was a Pillar Member of.

The Circle was illusive, secret and most of all careful in dealing with their matters of interest in and around Resheen, as well as other more out of the way places within The Shift, too; Redstone, Seacliffe, Briarstone, Marsham, Nasperine.

'They approached me with an offer,' I declared taking my empty glass to the bar and refilling it with Bourbon. 'You were the only person who bothered to tend my wounds and help me gain my strength, but all of this time I never knew why, until now.'

Michael walked forward and joined me at the mini-bar where I topped up his glass, too. The slow swig that he gave to the glass was a pause for thought, maybe to evaluate and validate my statement.

'You have gained the upper hand over your Cousin, Melissa, my Brother. The Circle in its wisdom may find your support a little more…'

'***They marked me!***' I cried, drinking back the whole entire contents of the glass and again filling it up. 'They marked me for the act of which I do not yield to admit being a crime or sin, but one of love. Now I have nothing…except a fucking cursed house in the middle of a damned family feud!'

My anger showed only too well to Michael.

'What did they look like?' He asked, having me wrack my brains to remember the description of a man that I already knew, and who I was once very well connected with.

I nodded my head from side to side slowly. 'Does it matter?'

Michael was so sure in his mind that it did, though the pain he was indicating manifested itself from his very own knowing that once a person was "Marked" by The Circle, there was no coming back from it.

'Like I said, she'll be the death of you, Brother!'

Making his short, somewhat cryptic excuses before leaving, I showed him out into the forecourt entrance. It was then just when I was about to wave him off, that the Evermore Police pulled up from the driveway to disperse in a strange manner, until they saw Michael sitting in his car watching them.

'Would you mind exiting the vehicle, Sir, just a routine check, nothing to worry about.' One of the Police Officer's, Douglas Flood, said walking over to Michael's car with a steady hand on his pistol tucked away in the holster. 'I won't fucking ask you again!'

The loud dry tone, almost insubordinate attitude fused itself together with the Draconian and Bohemian cowardice traitor.

'Then do not ask, if not answered, it shall not matter.' He was suddenly quoting "The Song Bird" in quite a defiant manner.

Giving him a round of applause, three burley Police Officers were given the nod from Flood, who proceeded to rush at me with great speed and only one thing on their little tiny minds – to inflict as much pain possible before incarcerating me again in a small caged prison somewhere distant. Or, quite simply just kill me!

Michael was well aware that I was more than healed, giving him the opportunity of surprising the Officers with a little show of force; taking one of the Officers by the back of his neck and pulling them away until finally slamming him to the ground with a familiar sound of snapping bones.

'***You dare come to my home and exercise this shit!***' I roared out with anger. 'I demand that you step down and piss off!'

Sergeant Ronald Flood was a family man, with his remaining Officers who were probably the same, except for one who looked like he didn't even know what a family was. It was with the tarnished, warm gold wedding band on his finger that merely suggested he had seen it all; the miraculous birth, the beautified wife – or Lover – who goes from the hour glass figure to Molly Winters proportion in less than four months after becoming a Mother. But it is still that thought of "Once was" that could unhinge the Officer and have him yield to my authority.

'Just doing our job, Lord Lucas, you know how it is?' Flood spoke up, his intelligence insulted so much that he had stepped closer to my stance.

Tutting several times I turned to Michael, and then, without the slightest hesitation I turned quickly back to Flood.

'Your wife…!' I begged his other half's name.

'***Rosie Lee…I don't understand!***' He gasped with worry.

'Rosie Lee, Okay, and the kids…how many?'

The ice breaker had started and Michael knew that it could work, especially if I was a true Overseer of Evermore – or the closest thing to it. Flood pondered on the answer, his face showing great concentration in his eyes as he searched every nook and cranny in his head to find the names of his five children.

'There's Robert, Stanley, Thomas, Jack and Jenny, of course, all at college now though,' he finally replied with a show of pride on his face. 'Jenny turns nineteen tomorrow, so the money from this job will pay for her…!'

Realizing he had said too much he bowed his head. 'I'm sorry, Lord Lucas, but this is for your own good. Plus, you'll be helping Jenny out so much, too, I'm sure she will appreciate it?'

In the skip of a heartbeat the Officers, Michael and me began to clash violently. Blood, teeth, mucus and spit flew one way to the next unconscious Officer awaiting those that Michael droned to the floor like paper-weights. The two that I was left to deal with were pretty good with their mouths, very poor with their fists, however, and just as clumsy on their feet.

The Workout, as Michael referred to it, lasted only several minutes before Frobisher and several heavily armed Private Security Guards came rushing out of the Manor House and surrounded both me and Michael.

Eyes Of A Stranger

Instructing Frobisher to release Michael immediately, he gave a wave to the guards and stood almost to attention before me with a face like a wet weekend. Something was definitely on his mind – and it definitely wasn't a body count.

'What is it, Frobisher? What is it that you want to ask me?'

Frobisher was a man of principle, honor and above all loyalty.

'You're Cousin, Lady Melissa Ellington-Evermore, Sir,' he began to ask, observing my reaction. 'We would like to have your permission to bury her here, in the grounds of Evermore, so that your next generation will be enriched in the…!'

I waved at him to stop speaking. 'Yes.'

Frobisher stopped, he looked right at me with a tockteric stare that told me he was not only very loyal to my Cousin, he was actually very loyal to her service, too; as all Personal Assistants were given the task of laying their former employer, friend – even Lover in some cases – to rest.

Excusing himself from mine and Michael's company, we stood watching him and his men head back to the house and quickly disappear back inside. The leaving of the Officer's was left up to us to sort out, as I scratched my head while looking down at them all lying on the ground.

'I remember both your Mother's, Michael's especially, however! They used to call her Kirstie Curtains…'

Michael bit to Flood's pathetic little mind game, one which he had no way of winning. Don't misunderstand me, he was strong, fast and elixired to the max. But what he gained in brawn and brute force, he lacked in knowledge and discipline.

'You talk about my Mother like she's some kind of whore, you sick cunt! I'll have your fucking heart beating its last in the palm of my hand by dawn tomorrow, Flood!'

Sure, Michael warned him. Flood though, he changed his game plan to one that I was unfortunately drawn to the act of which redefined me as a Lord over an estate.

'And you, Lord bloody Lucas Cavendish, the Bastard son of an unfaithful Mother. You make me fucking sick, the lot of you. You're secret love with someone our boss doesn't like you being with, she must be some very cute fucking whore over there in Borello? I mean, who can blame you with the life you've had, growing up here and listening to all the rumors that are sent around.' Flood continued with hope in his voice that I was going to do something insane.

An intense moment of silence followed his harsh words, even

with his best shot at making me bend to the lies, my back was already covered. Flood was knocked out by Michael, who then ordered the rest of the Officers off the land. Fortunately, within minutes of moans and groans they took up their superior from off of the floor and carried him back to the vehicle before driving off at high speed.
Thanking Michael I threw him my car keys.

'You never know, leave yours here for now and come get it later...whenever your passing!' I shouted up, knowing only too well that if Michael took his own car he would be stopped before getting anywhere near Borello Town.

'I'll see you in Borello, Lucas...Lord of the Madhouse!' He joked jumping into my RCZ-R and driving away.

If I was to be honest, my decision to return to Borello was all that I could think about between the chit chat and hidings that I'd given those Officers, who were crooked, so I doubt that even counts as a static misdemeanor. Of course, there would be some blow-back from the dead Officer, and simply because that kind of violence was frowned upon throughout the whole of Resheen, as well as the rest of Chatandra, too.

'You're...Guest has gone, Sir!' Frobisher sounded out from behind me suddenly as I entered the lounge, scaring me slightly with a start.

'*Christ!* Frobisher, don't do that, I could have hurt you!'

He apologized sincerely for the surprise, but had a look of doubt beaming a restrained smile that actually annoyed me, but not as much as his off-the-cuff bold statement.

'I very much doubt that, Sir, you see, our training exceeds that of Butler. By "Exceeds", I do mean other than opening doors and helping people off of the premises, if I may speak frankly, Sir?'

I was Gobsmacked. Here was a man who I had always imagined being someone with a big stick stuck up his arse and not even slightly Kick-Ass as Captain Price, but that day at my home in Evermore, I started to see a completely different side to everyone, Frobisher especially – myself included.

'That's...That's a pretty impressive claim that you are making,

considering, of course!' I said with a calm smile.
Frobisher put a poised finger up in the air.

'If I may demonstrate my skills…as a means of a test, Sir?'
This was sounding more and more like a 'Contest', rather than a demonstration that would show me exactly what Frobisher was. Nevertheless, I was willing to see his efforts and maybe along the way, he could pick up some of my techniques.
The Knight's Castle; an important House in The House of Houses, which enlisted the best minds and agilities that any man – or woman - had to offer.
Frobisher removed his jacket, undid the buttons on his cuffs and finally stood before me with his hands by his sides.

'Just say when you're ready, Sir!' Frobisher offered the start of this demonstration over to me.
As soon as I said "Okay", it was on. With a fast hard lunge at my chest while he sank to his knees, I was knocked back into the center of the room. He had a tough punch.

'*Apologies, Sir, I didn't mean to…!*'
Stopped with a calm wave I steadied myself while shaking off the energy draining strike and its painful residue.

'That's Okay, Frobisher, it was a move I was not expecting.'
Frobisher bowed slowly. 'Indeed, Sir, will that be all?'
For the life of me I didn't know how else to address this, it was as if he was actually talking me down, negotiating the terms so to speak, though he as the 'Winner'.

'Actually, Frobisher, maybe one more demonstration would actually break it, so to speak!' I replied taking off my jacket.
Accepting the invitation, as Frobisher put it, we locked in combat for nearly ten minutes; arms, legs, noses and even ears were cut, sliced, bruised and broken during the fight of true Warrior style Hand-to-Hand Combat by this man that I was in the process of sacking. He was better than very good, he was superb, fast, intelligent and more than an asset I could not lose from Evermore Manor.

'Congratulations, Frobisher, you have the job.' I informed him with a pained smile and outstretched hand for him to shake. 'Just know the rules, after nightfall, I will not need your services, do we understand one another?'

Giving a nod he thanked me for resuming his employ at the Manor House, and then he set about his routine and chores.

That evening, as soon as the sun went down and the sound of The Sheekan's made their after eight calls, I snuck out of the Manor House and across the back Orchard's to Riverside. It was here that I had a small place on the very edge of the village, quiet and secluded enough to allow me privacy.

'Good evening Lucas?' The village Priest, Father Roman, shouted over to me passing the security gate to the grounds as I was entering. 'It's a beautiful night, isn't it?'

Father Roman was a man not that different from Father Benedict in Borello, his stance on the whole upset caused by the wars between both Evermore and Borello was a simple one – to drop our weapons and make peace. Sometimes I wondered if his prayers were actually being answered, as he was an ordained Priest of The Paroxinate League; a Secret Order of some great measure that oversaw many menial jobs with those in positions to use their services, something similar to the likes of The Lexicon, only much bigger, wiser and more better equipped to deal with anything – or anyone who meant them harm.

'Father Roman, how good to see you out this fine night,' I greeted him a smile while climbing out of my car and walking over to the security box by the gate. 'I was just calling in to gather some clothes, would you like a cup of tea, Father?'

Giving a non-hesitant nod and loud anxious "Yes", I typed in the code and made my way back to the car while the gates clicked their unlocking sound and began to open.

'Hop in Father, it's quite a walk to the house.'

Father Roman got in, buckled himself up and sat back in his seat comfortably, or that's how he looked. Within moments we were pulling up outside the main entrance of the house.

'**So this is it!**' Father Roman whispered looking at the house in a way that he was expecting something a lot bigger.

'It's modest.' I said getting out of the car and walking up to the front door, Father Roman quickly following behind me.

Making our way into the house I lead my guest through into the kitchen, his face showing both glee and awe at all of the paintings, statues and other, more related items to a house of its historical caliber and ownership.

'Before I forget, Father, I do believe Mr. Frobisher will be in touch with you about a burial sometime soon,' I called out to him putting on the kettle and indicating a drinking hand, to which he nodded.

'A coffee please, Lucas, and may I ask who has died?'

My service to the Church, or be it The Paroxinate, was not all that secure. In fact, it was loosely based on an incident not so long ago, an argument – a disagreement, if you will.

'***My Cousin!***' I replied cryptically.

Father Roman tilted his head, as you do when reaching out or searching for more information. '***Oh My God!*** Which one?'

I held back my disrespectful laughter. 'Lady Evermore, of course, I don't consort with any of my other…Oh, hang on, yes I do, Lord Xander O'Neill.' I answered realizing that I had lost touch with so many people, Xander being one of the most important of them all. 'Could you make sure that it is done with respect, please, Father?'

He was absolutely shell shocked!

'***Lady Evermore! You're Cousin, Lady Evermore! She's dead!***' He gasped out a series of questions.

I left him to his thoughts while continuing making the hot drinks, and then when I had finished he was somewhat back with the living, but his manner and behavior was outward.

'The Masquerade Ball last night, she was cut down by The Borello Rogue…The Deadly Night Shade! My Cousin…me, even, nobody saw it coming – we just expected it to be later rather than sooner.' I informed him.

Pulling back his sadness, not in the loss of Lady Evermore, but in the whole damned business that had turned man against man in such a way, that he now had the sad duty of laying to rest the woman who ruled over the town of Evermore for more than thirty years.

'There will be repercussions, Lucas!' He sighed.

I knew already, but what was I to care? The Circle had already marked me for death, Elizabeth, too, under the Sovereign Law of Resheen, was already dead with the Sanction Order. These were strange days – strange times that would be somewhat very interesting in the coming months ahead.

'I have taken Succession, Father, something that I need to seek Counsel with The Order about and discuss renouncing it!' I told him by no other way than to emphasize something bad was coming to Evermore.

Shocked more than anything else he put on a brave face.

'The Order cannot give Counsel to…'

I had to stop him straight away from saying the one thing that had been said a million times before: The Order is for Servants of The Paroxinate only to seek an audience.

'There has to be another way, surely? Or in Borello, even?' I grabbed at a thought.

This was nothing to compare anywhere else with; without the personal invitation of The Order itself, there would be no point going through anyone else to get an audience.

Reassuring me that if there was anything further he could do to make it happen, he would let me know immediately, before he bid me a courteous farewell. Leaving the house and beginning on his way back down the well-lit drive on foot. In the meantime I'd checked my watch and realized that it was time that I wasn't there. Giving Father Roman time to leave the grounds I went into the study and looked out my clothes; not the normal attire which you would associate a Lord with, but garments of the utmost quality all the same.

The leathers were fine – tight fitting – adequately tailored by Rochelle's in Evermore Town, while the more private set of head wear was not done by anyone who would see a reward for their knowledge of my nightly activities. I was clothed and ready to leave for The Quarter, and in particular, it was going to be The Bastille Tavern where I was to bless my presence.

'I hope for your sake you're not in here on a job?' Molly sighed while pulling me a pint of House Ale. 'You still haven't sorted me out for that last lot of skulls you cracked together last week! It took me bloody hours to scrub the claret off that floor it did!'

Those skulls that Molly was referring to were my Cousin's own Private Guards, most probably the very same Private Guards that I would now have appointed to watch over me, protect me, kick the shit out of me and kill me, too, given half the chance. If there was one thing that Evermore Guards didn't do, it was forget a beating.

'Not tonight, Molly, I'm looking for…'

'***You've found him!***' A loud voice boomed from behind me. Turning around cautiously I set my eyes on Alistair Bishop, or to those of his victims in and around Borello Town, he was a Thief, just like me. By day he was Alistair Townsend, the spoilt son of a Lord, one who had the perfect cover of discretion.

'***Oh My God!*** Are you still breathing, Alistair?' I joked pulling him in closer to the bar so that we could talk and drink.

Alistair had been doing a little time in a Prison up North near the Nasperine Border, and had only been released that same day under a Sovereign Pardon no less!

'There's these people up there, some don't even have eyes! It's spooky, Lucas, and certainly no place for any man to be locked away.' He complained of his lack of freedom.

It was understandable that anyone living a life like we did, it being by day or night, the rules are set in ***their*** favor, not ours. There are rules, there are laws, there are regulations and there are conditions which we scrutinize with the utmost inspection. What does not change, what does not yield, nor surrenders in any easy manner is the fact: Crimes are punishable.

'So, how long did you get, Lucas?' Alistair asked me suddenly. The sheer surprise of the question knocked my concentration and even my attention to a small person who was at the time standing right behind my friend, listening in on our very private conversation.

'No, your mistaken, I wasn't as lucky as you, my friend. My Cousin sent me to The Farm, she thought a break would help me…Chillax a little more!' I laughed out loudly along with my friend, who was immediately knocked to the floor by a

swooping Beer Stein that smashed across the back of his head. Whether I was acting with instinct or by pure luck, my reaction was quick and relentless as I scanned the room to see where the attacker of Alistair was, and immediately giving chase.
Molly Winters the Barmaid watched over an unconscious Alistair while I made my pursuit of what looked like a small teenage boy dressed in Leatheral's and suede that were almost as good as mine, up through the rafters and onto the roof top before jumping several short spaced buildings onto the veranda of The Borello Bell Tower. This was no Target who had taken opportunity to render Alistair unconscious before robbing him, no, this was a setup – but for who, and for what? Slowing down and allowing the culprit to gain a 'Lost' sense of security for my chase, I rested up across from The Bell Tower and watched as the Thief I believed to be a boy, in fact turned out to be a woman – a very young woman, too. The longer I watched the more I was somehow amazed by her abilities used while in combat training with a tall man who I recognized as Father Benedict – the Borello Paroxinate.

'Her name is Jet!' Michael whispered from behind me, his voice far from being the first hint of his presence. 'She came here to Borello five years ago when she was just eleven with her Mother, became an Orphan shortly afterwards. She seeks Solitude and Training with Father Benedict, so that she has the means and skills to end the life of the one who killed her Mother.'
The story was interestingly stereotypical of those many other lives that shared the same brunt and scathing's that happen here in Borello, after all, if Fate, Destiny or Death were biased or discriminating against anyone, I'd not seen it of late.

'She's a kid in Borello, who is out to kill someone, even at her age? Still, she must be punished and shown discipline for her actions…'

'Like you and I, you mean? Come on, Lucas, Alistair most probably deserved it!' Michael said standing in my way of jumping over onto the very same veranda that the girl had used to gain entry into the Church Tower.

'So what if it would have been you, Michael?' I said pointing blindly in an attempt of an alternative example.

He laughed at me. He annoyed me.

'I'm sorry, Lucas,' he choked his pause of laughter to calm himself down. 'I would not be so fucking stupid as to get hit over the head by a fifteen-year-old in the first place! Come on, or are you saying I'm slow?'

Michael had a point. It did sound pretty condescending in its delivery, while the two examples didn't necessarily need to be referral's to anyone in particular. Michael would have been a true gentlemen in his apprehension of the young girl, who was not fifteen, but sixteen going on seventeen.

'Are you being serious right now?' I gasped with disbelief.

Lowering his temper at my utter dismay of the situation, he sat down on the roof tiles behind him and folded his arms.

'Is she why you came back tonight, to hunt down and give a good spanking? Let it go, Lucas and let's go find something more sporting...like that woman whose staring at us both right now over there!'

Michael's gaze glared right through me, or so it seemed. His eyes were glossed over with sedeal and carandur due to his recent visit to The Knight's Castle, no doubt to indulge in the delightful offerings of The Opium Emporium until he was as straight minded as the escaping soul who lived in pretense of his body.

'***That looks like Shade!***' I gasped a loudening whisper that alerted the dark shadowy figure that just stood there near the chimney stack looking down on us.

'***Elizabeth!***' Michael called out at the figure. '***Is that you?***'

The figure pushed a hand into their cloaked hoodie and grabbed what looked like a weapon of some kind, a gun maybe, we couldn't be sure. Immediately, Michael took out a handgun and pointed the laser dot sight at the dark figure, an action that saw the loaded weapon in his hand being lassoed and taken from his grip. Michael was not happy that he had been disarmed.

'***Yield Rich Blood!***' The figure called down while unloading the handgun of its bullets and then threw it back down to a stunned Michael.

'Why didn't she use the weapon on us?' He gasped.

I knew why. The weapon we thought it to be in their hand was a remote detonator – to what exactly we had no idea – that was primed and ready to be initiated. The figure pressed the button. Without any hesitation I turned, stepped forward and built up speed into a run before clashing into Michael, knocking us both off of the roof and into the watery depths of the Chorim River below. A moment later the entire building we had been standing on, along with the dark figure exploded with a thunderous blast so tremendous that it rendered both Michael and me completely unconscious with the shockwave.

The Borello Kiss

The "Leap of Faith", as Michael liked to call it, was neither a leap, nor a part of any Faith. Truth be known, what we had done to escape the explosion of the building was reckless on our part. Even so, however, we had survived both the impact of the freezing Chorim River waters and failed to drown, so all in all, I guess we were lucky.

Waking to the smell of burning meat or some form of flesh to flame was filling the air that I breathed. Lifting my head slightly up in the air I managed to see four…five people who were sitting around in chairs, Michael was already conscious and talking with them quietly.

'This Night Shade character has been the fall of many man – and woman, to be fair, Master Michael…'

'Has there been any confirmation on her identity?' Michael asked turning and looking over toward my weak, tired waking body. 'Hang on a second, looks like Lucas here is awake!'

Rushing over to my side and helping me to my feet, I looked across the room into the eyes of a well-known Borello Police Officer, his slight scare upon seeing me was clear enough to everyone. Michael told him to relax.

Jackson Keltman was a man of many bad things, both currently and previously. If anyone in that room had no damn right calling the kettle black, then it was Keltman. His thirst for money, wealth, fortune and power was all that drove him.

'But, he's The…!'

'He's my friend, and he needs to rest, Jackson, come on man, take the day off being a twat and give me a hand?' Michael cried out walking me to a nearby chair before resting me down. Getting one of the other Officers to get me a drink of water from the other room, Keltman took out a packet of cigarette's and offered me one; a Woodbine kind of cigarette that had been well packed with strong tobacco that on the very first drag had me coughing slightly.

'This life you and your friend are leading…it has to stop!'

Michael for one was in no way surprised by the Officer's sudden statement, an insulting statement at that.

'Why, have they got you working for your wages now, Keltman? You worry about the job in hand and how much they pay you to get it done. The girl, how close are they to getting confirmation?' Michael blasted at the Officer.

Keltman drew out his reply, most probably while in two minds whether or not to share any information with Michael. But, with a deep long sigh he finally gave us the answer we needed.

'The girl is, as yet unidentified. That's why they've brought in reinforcements…'

'**Reinforcements!**' Michael probed quickly.

The Enforcers of Redstone, Briarstone and of course the small town of Nasperine had been assigned the job of "Ridding" the plague of Vigilante types in and around Borello, especially that of The Borello Hood and The Deadly Night Shade.

'They brought them in when Aaron Jones turned up two days ago, he has a signed Sanction to kill you on sight Kid, and he looks the type who enjoys his work, too.' Keltman replied, his voice sounding all for one on the Lawmen, while suddenly realizing that this could be bad for him and his corrupt cops too, if it was to be put into effect.

There it was, the news that we had both been expecting from

the low and silent whispers passing through the streets of every town, city and region throughout Resheen. This was no small threat of the law tracking down, arresting and sending to prison two fugitives, it was an execution-style Witch Hunt.

'Jones, isn't he the one who worked with Warren Jackson?' The name sounded so familiar to me, the Aaron Jones of Redstone was considered "Warrior" type. Once, one of his captors attempted to escape from his holding, until he was found with no head on his shoulders. Jones had connected a device of some kind to the wanted man's neck, which was programmed to detonate a small charge of P4 explosive when the restraint reached two hundred yards from the transponder.

'Warren Jackson, you say?' Keltman spoke up before Michael could answer. 'The Jackal of Redstone. Now that's one hard bastard there. According to Flood's memo, it was Jackson who signed off the contract on you and that whore running around the town...'

Keltman was quickly rubbing his jaw and counting his teeth on the floor before Michael tore us apart of one another, his eyes showing some unfathomable rage that could only be obeyed.

Keltman wasn't worth the hassle, nor the effort in trying to teach him new manners, either. There was a feel of unsurities.

'One more fuckin' stunt like that and I'll take you in myself!' Keltman warned stepping back away from me angrily.

Deciding to get out of there while the coast was clear, Michael led us through The Bordello Tunnels, down the deep trenched subsystem of winding pipes, tubes and hidden enclaves that had been adapted by the Dweller's. This was a place where only the strongest survived, while those weaker were torn to pieces by the more organized and cruel minded among the vagrants and lost. It was a horrible place.

'Where are you taking me, Michael?' I asked stopping to catch my breath. 'What is this place?'

Seeing that I had stopped he returned to me with an agitation that could be read as jittery, but was certainly not fear.

'We can't stop here, Lucas...'

Suddenly, there were several men surrounding us with

primitive weapons held fast in their hands. A tall man standing above us near the walkway on the surface held out a hand and pointed at Michael with a mad smile.

'***You!*** I'll take you,' he growled as the others raised their laughter while cheering their leader on.

The men were Chorim Urchers, the sort you did not want to engage in combat with – on any level. They were mixed of their cultures, as well as their abilities; made up mostly of those refugees made homeless by the war, others being the soldiers left out in the cold and shunned by both sides. They were most probably good people before they went off to war, though both Michael and myself knew that some things witnessed were so horrific, even stupefying your brain day in, day out couldn't take the haunting screams away.

'***You challenge me!*** ' Michael laughed out loudly. 'I assure you, come closer my crazy friend and I will rip the very heart from your chest and feed it to a Borellian Meest!'

The Urcher didn't seem to be afraid. '***Rich Blood!*** Should be a lot of meat on those well fed bones!'

Even if the crazy fucker was right in his assumption, I was getting bored with the whole thing, as was Michael, too. Reaching for my handgun I extended it out to target the man.

'***STOP!*** ' A loud scream echoed around the subsystem.

The voice was effective, more than it would have been if it was from either of us shouting. The Urcher's quickly lowered their weapons and disbanded, disappearing into wherever it was they came from, while the leader stayed with a firm concentrated eye on Michael. It was only moments later when the woman who had called out made her way toward us – it was Shade.

'These be mine and the boys, Shade, not your property!' The leader informed her with a demanding tone in his voice.

Elizabeth – The Deadly Night Shade – turned around to me with a blank look.

'These men are here to kill me, Adrock, but they know nothing of this world down here. Tell me, do you really believe that you can take this one here?' She whispered coldly pointing at Michael.

Adrock was from The Island, not here in Resheen, which in some way or another gave Michael the overall advantage. He knew Borello like the back of his own hand or so he told me during my recovering months back at The Square.

'It would seem that your girlfriend here has turned into a first class bitch! Give it your best shot, Odrick!' He cried purposely mispronouncing the leaders name.

'Stupid Rich Blood, I am Adrock Teal, Odrick is my brother!' There were no guesses at trying to fathom out the chances of that happening, but for the record it worked out the wrinkles in the situation.

'You do know that I'm not a Rich Blood, right?' Michael turned and declared to Adrock's confused looking face.

Elizabeth encouraged the outsider with a glare. 'Well?'

Rushing at Michael with speed Adrock dove through the air and landed a bare flat foot across my friend's chin, and of course he went down. This was to be the very first and last time my friend was going to see the darkened soil of the sewers in his face.

'Alright then, now you've made me angry!' Michael joked out as Adrock made a second pass on him, one which had Michael turn quickly and snap punch the Urcher straight in his face.

Elizabeth moaned a sigh before starting to walk away from the grounded Adrock Teal, whose throat was now being throttled by a furious Michael. I found it hard to choose which to watch over, which to follow, which to help.

Giving in to helping my friend out, I ran up to both him and Adrock, pulling Michael away while at the same time kicking an unconscious blow to the Urcher's chin. Obviously my friend was angry, I had put to sleep the one person he didn't.

'I had that handled, Lucas!' Michael blasted at me angrily.

'Handled! In what way did you have that handled, Michael? You're upper hand snap was sloppy, you only just managed to get the thick cunt down!' I shouted back at him defiant of his threatening manner and behavior.

Nodding his head from side to side, he looked at me strangely.

'This woman, Elizabeth, does she know you love her, Lucas?'

I nodded slightly before stopping and looking just as strange.

'I...I don't know!' I replied quietly enough for him to hear.

As far as I could tell from Shade's last encounter, there was no sign of the Elizabeth I had fallen in love with. That black soulless ocean that crashed around deep in her eyes was enough to confirm the former tenant had now Checked Out.

'You two need to follow me...'

'To where? Where are we going?' Michael asked suddenly.

Elizabeth put up a shushing finger to her lips, something that rattled Michael's cage all the while we were following the woman I had searched for these past several months.

'Or stay here, either way, I don't give a shit!' She responded with a low-kick at the ground before continuing on her way up through a winding tunnel toward a zirconic orange glow.

'This used to be the topside of Borello; the buildings, the lawns, streets and fields. The war from Evermore came at a bigger price than death, it brought the separation of the people and what they stood for in this town.' Elizabeth started to tell us the story of how the Subsystem Enclave was created.

According to many, the two towns in conflict made each their foundations weaker with day and night bombings that never seemed to stop. Under the surface of Borello, as it is rumored of Evermore, too, subsystems running from one end to the other have been prepared for more than a hundred years.

'As you well know, the death of Lady Evermore, has left the whole balance in a state of flux!'

Michael dared to near Elizabeth, a move that saw her turn and throw out a hand for him to stop.

'Right where you stand is where Aaden Luxton the first man of Borello Town tended his very last stand during the first war. It is said that he knew only too well that he was about to fall in the bloodiest of all battles against Evermore, but even so, he never gave in to surrender his fate.' She said before turning again and walking on. 'My Mother, Susan Spinks, was a woman of passion, kindness and respect...respect that was thrown back at her!'

Though I never really knew her Mother before Alice cut her

throat in front of scores of witnesses, I could but repeat my previous condolences for her loss. And it was this that had her change – slightly.

'You were a good friend to me, Lucas, one that my Mother saw good in too, and yet, you still remain the same person who was to blame!' She whispered into a cry. 'And you, Michael, the one man Alice hung on for all this time while you were away in that American Prison. Did her fairytale ending become that of your blame, too?'

Elizabeth was not talking about past guilt's or crimes against the people we knew and loved, but of the now. This was a speech that had all the hallmarks of a trial viciously watching us both walk the 'Dead Mile'; three miles of reflection, while the final few feet would see us grabbed, disrobed and beheaded. It was that quick in practice as it was in explaining.

'I sacrificed my life for you, Elizabeth, don't you remember? When you wanted to have your revenge right there and then, but for Alice sparing you and your family…'

'*Family!* If you knew what that cunt did to me, you would look at yourself with shame and humiliation the whole day through! The doctors, the nurses, surgeons and master brains in fixing the wealthy, the strong and the rich. They made sure that my Family had no chance to continue walking this Earth!'

My mind was so wrapped up in the ways of Borello and those of Evermore, that somehow, somewhere, I had become lost of the compassion in which I swore I would never lose to the ways and means of The Evermore Family Bloodline. Also to the fact that Alice Gruber had inadvertently, but knowingly put to death the Soul of Elizabeth, who secretly or passively fell in love with me five years ago. Her banishing from Evermore by my Cousin sent up the very first red flag, and then the time I spent in The Institute. She was angry – Shade was angry.

'Melissa is dead, the hurt is over, we must move on with our lives, Elizabeth,' I whispered in an attempt to calm her.

Elizabeth did not speak, she just bowed her head down to the ground and thought for a few moments. It was an action that had Michael looking over at me with a hinting shift of his eyes for me to go over and comfort her in her sadness. But she was neither sad or in need of comforting.

'I want…I need…!' She paused purposely to turn around and look down the path we had just walked to see a dark figure that moved within the shadows. 'What exactly is it that you want?'
The question, to me personally, was one that she already knew the answer to. I guess for Michael it was different, but almost the same shared quest that was now nearing the end of its journey.

'Courtesan Elizabeth, that's what he wants Sweetheart!' Michael cried out after a long few moments of silence that had him scratch his head with impatience and most probably that of boredom, too.
Elizabeth nodded her head from side to side. '**Watch your fucking mouth!** As for you, the Elizabeth you once knew is no more…'
This was not a negotiation. '**Oh no!** My eye sights pretty good since The Institute, and I say you look like Elizabeth to me.'
My shouting made her step back, almost into a stance of combat, but then relaxed to stride her way toward me.

'Don't do this,' she whispered softly diverting her eyes from my looking into hers. 'there is no way this can happen.'
'*But I…!*' My mouth was shushed with a sudden kiss upon my quivering lips.
For almost a whole minute I was locked in a kiss that made me crumble – completely, and immediately. The sensation was so intense that I failed to see the group of soldiers take up their positions close to where we were stood, making good of our time together so they could concentrate their sights on two easy targets.

'*Hands up!*' A man shouted out firing a gunshot into the air. It was Officer Flood and Adrock Teal with at least twenty well-armed men, enough to keep both Michael and me busy for a few minutes, give or take. The three of us put our hands up.
'***Flood, you have this bad habit of crossing my path!*** ' Michael spoke up taking a step forward, his attempt met with a single bullet to the leg, just above the knee cap, but just as

equally painful. '***SON-OF-A-BITCH!***'
The actions against Michael were certainly not stupefied by the idea of getting away with something that Lady Gruber would never forgive them doing, but, simply a genius idea for Flood and the soldiers to present as evidence against the young Libertine who had escaped their grasp so many times before but with no firm evidence to give in their case.

'You wander a path that will never allow you peace!' Elizabeth exclaimed with a dead cold stare at Flood and the one man she herself saved on more than one occasion. 'You will have no place to hide anymore Adrock.'

Flood calmed Teal down from taking a shot at Elizabeth by taking his weapon and unloading the bullets, the actions which were met with a threat of sorts.

'You forget where you are Resheenian, this is the Subsystem, the last place you ever want to push your luck, Commander!'

It was a blatant threat that Flood took with absolute force.

Pointing his gun at Teal's temple, Flood pulled the trigger. It was done instantly, without remorse or regret.

'***What the fuck!***' I cried out, an instant feeling – more of a knowing – that this was no official line of capture, but, one that could result in all our deaths without as much as a trial.

'Secure this trash and get them in the vans.' Flood gave his orders to the soldiers with a satisfied smile.

Elizabeth helped Michael to his feet, while I was pushed in the direction of a large customized Transporter Van, its side door opening as we approached to show two armed men guarding several steel cages that would be our holding cells for the entire trip into Borello. And by the markings on the sides it was privately ran by whoever Flood had brought in from elsewhere.

An Escape Plan Rouse

There were many things that Michael could have been called in those days of Borello Nights and Evermore Days, and stupid was not one of them. His experiences outside Resheen were as flavored and varied as mine were by the same degree, the only difference being, of course, my experimentation in being the people's symbol of hope and change had resulted in a lot of people being killed – more good people than bad, however.

'That Guard there, the one with the chubby belly,' Elizabeth whispered loud enough for *that* Guard to hear her. 'We'll take him by surprise and then take his keys, weapons and clothes!'

At first I was naïve to the fact that what was being said, was a rouse of trust and safety; psychologically, my first thoughts were of attacking the Guard somehow, while one or both my friends looted his unconscious body. This was exactly what Elizabeth wanted the Guard to think.

'No, we'll cut his throat and then take his weapons and clothes…except the blooded ones, of course!' Michael added in a loud whisper that brought a reaction.

Quickly rushing to the cage where Michael sat nursing his wounded leg, the Guard smashed a fist against the steel vented meshing. It was this that in its action weakened the doors main support by loosening the security bolt holding the lock.

Again, both Elizabeth and Michael set up another attack.

'Obviously he hasn't had a shag for a while, with a slap like that, I'd hazard a guess that he's gay!' Michael whispered with a hard suppressed urge to laugh.

'Actually, I don't think he's got any balls, because Borello Soldiers have their balls cut off! It makes their arse fucking that little more enjoyable…'

This did the trick. The Guard, now infuriated with the comments he'd overheard now growled out as he rushed at the mesh door, and just as he was right outside it, Michael let loose with a kick that sprang it open into the Guards face. At first he looked like he was dazed, until snapping out of it and grabbing a hold of Michael's feet. Dragging him out onto the ground, he began punching the wounded captive in the chest, ribs and face. But all the while, Michael held out until he found that one vulnerable advantage that would favor him over the Guard.

Standing to his feet the Guard towered over Michael with a hand gun pointing into his face.

'Don't fucking m...!'
Raising a powerfully charged shin high up into the air and into the Kaki material that covered flesh and bone, it struck its target with very painful consequences to the Captor. Immediately losing consciousness the Guard twitched his finger on the trigger of the gun, firing a bullet blindly and aimlessly through the air. In that intense moment, nobody knew where that bullet was heading.

The second that the Guard hit the ground Michael was up on his feet, limping over to both Elizabeth and me before releasing the locks on our cages.

'Is everyone... ***Oh shit!***' Michael greeted us both with a gasp at seeing that the bullet had found a vulnerable target in Elizabeth's shoulder. 'Pick her up and follow me.'

Michael wasted no time in getting the weapons from the Guard's unconscious body on the ground and preparing himself to burst through the back doors of the van. And, with a shot at the first man who approached him, then a second at a soldier who was shouting down at him from behind a Wheelie Bin that hid his head. For the moment the coast was clear of shooters, but whether it was clear enough for us all to escape, that was another matter which Michael had also thought of.

'Take her somewhere safe, Lucas, then both of you make yourselves disappear!' He shouted out checking his ammo and taking up a position back by the van.

I was in a Flux; my legs surging with an energy drawn from the quickened adrenaline that coursed through my entire body at tremendous speed. The feeling inside me had me believe that I was invincible, untouchable and unstoppable. All the same I carried Elizabeth's injured body from the van back into the town of Borello, down into The Subsystem, and finally found the lair in which she had been hiding out. As soon as we entered, her body was taken from me by three men who took her to a nearby makeshift bed.

'She has lost a lot of blood, Brother Lucas!' One of the men said with a sad, but assuring smile. 'The bullet has followed through, which means, she will live. But she will need lots of rest. You, too, must rest.'

They were words that I was praying to hear someone say as they set to work on stopping the bleeding and stitching her up. It was becoming light outside as Elizabeth coughed and asked for water to dry her parched lips, to which I took a dampened cloth soaked in clear fresh water before dabbing it gently across her lips. She looked so weak.

'Michael?' She whispered with difficulty.

I nodded my head slowly from side to side. 'I don't know.'

The look on her face told me everything; she felt trapped within the ties and bonds of her own true self, weak and also defenseless at the fact she could not search for or help our friend in any way.

'You have to…go and find him, Lucas, make sure he is…'

Elizabeth was too weak to speak anymore, her voice lowered and faded as one of the men approached me with a piece of paper in his hand.

'She needs rest Brother Lucas, you should take this and go home…back to Evermore.' He whispered before kneeling down by the side of Elizabeth to tend to her.

At first I thought he was trying to brush me off, until I looked at the piece of paper he had handed me. It was a name and address: Danielle La Grande, 185 Bastille Court, Borello.

'And this is…?' I asked turning to face the man with a blank expression of knowing nothing of the information.

'Elizabeth's hope of fulfilling her destiny, Lord Evermore, of course. The Lady who is not a Lady, may become the best of all Queens, or so they say.' He replied quite coyly.

What he said was the words to a Lullaby from my early years as a child, words that many people believed were from the lost verses of "The Evermore Song", as much as there was the famous song of "Borello", too.

'*Those words!*' I gasped.

Jumping to his feet the man put a gentle hand on my shoulder and told me to listen to him very carefully. I was to go to Bastille Court and find the young woman, and once I had found her I was to bring her back to The Subsystem where they would all be waiting for our return. I nodded with my confirmation before leaving for the Topside of Borello.

To Replace A Queen

The way to 185 Bastille Court was taken through the short strays and undersides of the buildings, eventually reaching The Spire and Bordello Church, I mingled with the crowd of other publicans who went about their business. Stopping outside the small North Gable book shop on the Main Street, I gazed across the road to a Tailor's Shop that bore the name Isla Vientan, who was one of the best in the business for likeable clothing and attire.
Making my way inside I was greeted by an old woman, her dress of importance, though casual in a way that had me give a second look and warm smile.

'Ah, The Marquis of Constantinople wear, may I ask where it was that you acquired such fine clothing, Sir?' She asked as if never seeing silk woven shirts or Leatheral breeches before.

'Robinson and Hartley, Evermore. I am looking for a more fitting appearance, maybe something of a Borello theme!' I returned my answer to her temporary puzzled stare.

'Borello theme! You wish to be dressed and seen in the light, as if hiding in the darkness, either way, my fabrics will make you the star of the night.'
The woman was well and truly into her own profession, as in a moment of describing the type of attire I wished to be seen in, she set to work pulling garments and fabric rolls from one small shelf to the next, before sitting down at a sewing machine humming another familiar tune – It was The Borello Song.
The twenty minute wait inside the Tailor's Shop passed quickly, the morning outside was already calling to the numerous workers who walked by. In a loud soothing voice the old woman handed me a pile of clothes and pointed to a nearby changing room that consisted of a hole in the wall and a

short drop curtain for privacy.

'Do not forget to check your collar, it may need adjusting, but if I am correct in guessing your neck size, it should fit you like a glove.' She announced as I walked over to the room and shut the curtain behind me.

Inside I looked around at the peeling paint from the walls, the wet stained floor that showed wood rot and rising damp. In the far left corner there was a tall fixed wall mirror, by the side of this a collage of photographs, one in particular caught my eye; the old woman along with three others stood for a pose while outside a large brown bricked building. One of the three others was Elizabeth, and it had been taken quite recently.

Taking off my Leatheral pants I stood half naked whilst with a second look at the mirror I noticed I had lost some weight around my mid-drift area, and in turn deserved a little pat of the hand across the stomach bulge. Looking lower I saw that my cock was hanging down, the softened semi-erection making the white silk shirt I was still wearing seem dated somehow.

'What do you look like?' I whispered at my reflection.

Continuing to disrobe myself of the shirt I finally picked up from the pile of clothes the old woman had handed me a pure black Valencian Molchen Shirt and pants that had been made from the same material, it felt exquisite as it touched my bare naked skin. Faring well with the selection and choice that the woman had given me, I returned to her by the counter.

'***And the neck!*** ' She exclaimed suddenly while I was busy adjusting the cuffs.

'Oh, yes, fine. Thank you.' I answered after receiving a sudden start that had me move my head away from the till. 'A very good guess.'

The woman chuckled while totaling up the cost of the clothes.

'Call it fifty straight…unless you would like to trade?'

Surprised by her forwardness, I gave a forced concerned smile that she immediately picked up on.

'The shirt and Leatheral's, I will give you twenty cash and swap you for the clothes you're wearing for the rest. Have we got a deal?'

Admittedly, it was a very good deal, one which could not have come at a better moment as I had no money. I nodded and put out a hand that was grasped and shaken vigorously.

Leaving happily from the shop I made my way back across the street and repositioned my watchful eye over the apartment. And it was only a few minutes later that I saw a figure open the veranda doors for a young woman to step out into the rising sun that covered the top half of the building with radiance. The woman was caught right in the mantrissic orange beams of the sun; she reveled in it, reaching her arms up above her head, as if yawning, but instead reaching for the heated rays that surrounded her in the sheer white negligée that she wore half open. She looked aglow and beautiful.

Without delay I rushed over to the apartment buildings main door and walked straight through to the enquiring sound of a man sat in the corner of the foyer, his face weathered and old, scarred in places, while on his laughing actions I saw he had lost all of his teeth. He looked like a tenant, though my best guess was that he was the building owner – or Manager.

'And where does you thinks you is going?' He shouted.

'That would depend on whose asking?' I replied, attempting to continue forward to the lift straight ahead of me.

Shaking his head he stood to his feet and approached me.

'Yous is not from around 'ere, are you, Kid? I is asking you where yous thinks yous is going because I is the owner of this fine establishment. You want a room, it'll cost yous five per night, or if it's a quick shag with one of the girls, it'll be ten.'

He was annoying me at the five for the room. 'Right, so if I wanted to do something a little...you know, kinky!'

He laughed, boy did he laugh at the insult I was directing at him personally? I mean, this man before me was the residue of someone who, once upon a time in a previous life of torment and hell might actually have been someone. The only problem was, however, so was I.

'As long as it pays for the cleanings and perks, it'll be twenty, to yous...Manager Special.' He said with a disgusting vile smile that begged me to think nothing of the twisted shit he had seen, or even been a part of during his ownership of the residence. Yet this did not stop me from taking out the forty-five and pressing it firmly against his forehead. He stopped laughing and looked cross-eyed at the barrel.

'I is listening, if that's what you want? Ah, I gets it, how about I lick you're balls?' He began to negotiate in a way that made me feel even less likely to allow him to live.

'***Stop talking! Shut you're fucking mouth!***' I said grinding my teeth tightly together and quietly growling out my words.

He shut up and moved his eyes to the floor. 'Okay.'

Glancing around I made a quick check of the buildings front door to see if anyone had wandered in from the street. The way was clear enough for me to continue, and continue I had to in aid of returning the young woman back to the people in The Subsystem.

'Get in the back…go on, move,' I ordered him into the rear of the building where I found his whole apartment was like a pigsty – though I believe pigsty would have been giving much more credit than was due. '***Fuck me!*** How the hell can you live like this?'

The one mistake I could have made, I made by asking that one question where the answer was always the same: Hard Life. It was to me a load of bollocks!

'Now,' I whispered, 'sit down over there and go to sleep!'

The man looked totally confused. 'Go to sleeps! Yous mean like take me'sen a nap or somefink?'

He was so right in many ways. 'That's right, here, I'll show you the way.'

Instructing him to walk over to the chair where he was under the assumption he was going to sit, I reacted fast to knock him out before he could turn around and look at me. It was quick and painless – almost – to the man. It could have been a lot worse, especially if anyone else had made the same move on him, anyway. At least he was still alive – regret was to follow.

Leaving his unconscious body slouched over the chair I made my way back to the Reception and searched for the spare key that would open apartment 185, which I found in a locked cupboard behind a large draping black curtain. From here I made my way upstairs via the lift, of course, stairs are so overrated since the invention of those people hoists that lift ones whole body skyward or downward to ground zero.

Reaching the fourth floor foyer I scanned the first couple of door numbers to make sure I was in the right part of the building, but for some reason or another, the numbers on the doors didn't correspond with anything in the sense of numbers, as each consisted of strange symbols that meant nothing – what in the hell was this building?

'Allow us to show you the way, Sir?' A kind helpful voice called out, just as I was greeted with unconsciousness.

By the time I regained consciousness, the night had already set in, again, with the Moon's Luna beams lighting up the room where I was now sat tied to a chair. The Manager was over by the door, his hand nursing a cracking headache caused by the pistol grip of my gun, which of course he now balanced and threw to and fro in his free hands.

'Who are yous? Police? Government? No, yous is something else yous is, aren't yous?' He suddenly demanded knowing that I was now awake. 'Is yous an unhappy customer?'

I was relieved to hear him give me the options of labelling, in particular the latter, the most spontaneously responsive of all answers asked by a complete moron.

'Yes, that Babs you gave me a few nights ago with my friends, she wasn't giving out for nothing, Man. She was like fucking a pile of spuds, if you know what I mean…I want my money back!' I said falling into perfect character.

He looked at me for a long few seconds before turning away to look at the bedroom door with a fixation.

'Roses and Candy, Marmalade and Shandy, we all pick you up with the one we call Mandy!' He sang out as if forced to do so.

'**Shandy!**' I cried, 'Shandy, that was the one, she was shite in the sack, so I want my money back.'

Turning to face me again the old man started to wave the gun around recklessly, as if he was unaware that the hammer could be released at any given moment of his bad handling of the weapon. I had to warn him.

'***Does I looks stupid***? Does I really looks like one of those damned Resheenian's who harvest the good and feeds the bad? I is the man around 'ere, what I say goes and if it doesn't, yous gets one in the noggin. Now, again, who the fuck are yous, and what are yous doing breaking into my hotel like this?'

His demands were shallow, his temperament swayed and not in the least bit stable, while his courage was of self-glorified notes that he had me prisoner by the way of holding a gun – my gun.

'My name is unimportant, I am looking for a young woman who lives here in this apartment block…'

'***Shut up!***' He demanded running up to me with the gun and imitating striking me with it, as I had done to him earlier. 'Yous looks nothing like a Copper, so you must be…'

Suddenly there was the sound of footsteps from behind the door that the man had been staring at for so long, and then the door opened for the woman I had seen at the window outside.

'***He is The Bordello Hood!***' She revealed to my dismay.

Now the man had a very pleasing look in his eyes, those who know what a BDSM night of pure evil is, will without a doubt know exactly what was going through his mind at that time.

'And you are?' I shouted up to her, only for the man to hit me hard in the stomach with his right hand.

Raising a hand in the air I was pleased for the young woman to call him off and away from me, and approach me with a pretty vacant look that had the man look away from her.

'I am someone who knows quite a lot about you, Lucas of The Cavendish Family. Yes, I know who you are, and I know who you become once the Moon crosses the night sky in your home town of Evermore.' She revealed more about me.

It interested me to know the reason why she spoke of me like she did, even though there were no real evident facts she said or mentioned, except my own knowledge of my true identity.

'Okay, my turn, you are sloppy, you have no discipline, no compassion, and definitely no boyfriend!' I fired back at her.

The young woman was between words, totally and utterly, I had thrown her train of thought off its rails, and now she had to rethink her strategy.

'*Sloppy! No Discipline! No Compassion!*' She repeated in a warm but shouldering temper that seemed to flare up her nostrils.

'Well, there's definitely no boyfriend, but its…Yeah, I'll shut my mouth.' I conceded.

The woman saw this and stepped down herself, signaling for the Guards she had arrived and entered the room with to position themselves along the veranda's to lower their weapons until further notice.

'You fight in the Dark against the Darkness that is consuming you, not for anyone else, but for your very own means and personal retributions. Take the hand of a King and know that he is offering friendship, but draw your sword and know that from that day forward, you will be the enemy for once you were a friend. What do you want?'

The woman was darsinked of her learnings, misled by her own emotions and redirected in some way to a much different place as this town's stench of death and decay.

'You are a Paroxinate?' I gasped.

She was neither shocked, nor surprised by my knowledge.

'I am The Circle,' she replied.

'As I am The Light.' I added to her satisfaction with no control as to stop the answer coming out of my mouth.

Nodding her head to signal one of the Guards to come down into the room, the young woman made herself comfortable on a seat near the door she had just emerged from.

'There is a Mutual in Dragon Town who wishes to meet with you, his name is Dominic Cruvier, you will know him as The Ensort at The Knight's Castle. He will let you know what you must do next to take your true place here…but be cautious in your journey, Lucas, it has many treacherous roads.' She told me, her eyes showing a form of sadness.

'You mean Assassin's?' I gasped, the only thought that filled my mind at the time. She shook her head.

'A Lady has fallen, one shall rise, it is you who has to travel the road and make a Lady into a Queen. You have many

enemies, Lucas, many who would prefer seeing you dead!'
The woman was right, there were quite a few old enemies, and new ones, too, who wanted to see me in the ground.

'So, this Queen, is she at The Knight's Castle?' I laughed, the thought that a woman, no matter who she was or of what bloodline she belonged to, I knew she would never be there.

'You mock those who are trying to help you, and yet…I see now!'
Strangely enough, knowing that I had spoken a little disrespect at the woman, she didn't do anything besides nothing at all. With a weary hand waved in the air at the Guard, I was handed a another small piece of paper, only this time it had nothing but a symbol written in its center.

'What's this?' I asked the Guard.
He didn't answer me, he just took my gun from the building owner and handed it back to me, before escorting me out into the streets of Borello, where I saw the glimmer of the Moon disappearing over the roof tops of the town in front of me.

The Opium Emporium

Dominic Cruvier was a man of absolute respect and distinction within Borello Town, while liked by everyone, hated by a few in his line of personal pleasurable business. To many he was simply The Whore Trader, to the people of Borello he was a man who tolerated no problems, as to the rest who frequently made their presence there it was home.

The Opium Emporium was adjacent to The Knight's Castle of Borello Town, coincidence bringing the two together as if it was meant to be, perhaps! Two prominent buildings that stood solo against each other's horizons and shadows.

'You must be Lucas?' Ensort Cruvier guessed who I was as soon as I walked through the doors, but calculating the odds on it being someone he didn't know gave me the hint that I was neither invisible nor discreet.

'Yes, and you are…!'

'***Hey!*** Let's cut the shit, Kid, every damned Mother-Fucker in this whole town knows who I am…and I know you do, too! You're here because they sent you, so do me a favor and shut the fuck up!' He roared out walking over to a lowered pure white sofa before sitting down rubbing his fingers around his temples to calm himself down. This guy was stressed out.
Pushed gently forward by one of his Private Staff, I was shown to a seat across from Cruvier, who was now sat forward with his face in his hands. I guess he was thinking.

'A substance for our guest, Mr. Lyle, something that will of course loosen him up a little.' He called over to the man who had shown me to my seat. 'And find out where that little Bitch is hiding…I want her here five fucking minutes ago, Mr. Lyle!'
He wasn't happy, though the way he was jittering about in his seat and sighing heavily was one sure sign that he was either expecting trouble, or he was about to unleash trouble on someone else.

'***I don't…!***'

'***Take drugs!*** No, neither do I, just the controlled kind.' He laughed out jumping to his feet and walking over to a mini-bar behind the sofa. 'Don't worry, you're friend Michael Slattery, he will be joining us very shortly too, Lord Lucas Cavendish – and can you guess why?'
I was sitting with the thought of "Why" I was there, not of anything else that could be carried with the quest of answering questions. I had no idea why Michael was going to be there.

'Because you kidnapped him, maybe?' I whispered.
Ensort Cruvicr liked me, he said so while fixing himself a large Brandy, pausing briefly to offer me the same – which I refused. His whole manner was nothing that I had expected, but then, what I expected was a man in drag clinging to a Boudoir stick cigarette that had all the hallmarks of the legendary Liz Taylor. Now that I was face-to-face with him, however, he reminded me of my Father, Lord Ronald Cavendish IV.

'Cassandra didn't tell me you were a comedian!' He quipped as Mr. Lyle returned with a young woman in toe and spoilt his building sarcasm cascade of La-de-da bullshit. 'Ah, here we are, the lovely Danielle. According to my contacts, she was made an orphan at a young age, the typical heart breaking story. Now she works for me here, to pay for her freedom, of course!'

His attention now diverted to the young woman, who seemed to be pretty perturbed by Cruvier's advances toward her, I saw Mr. Lyle lean forward and whisper some unheard message in her ear. This in turn brought her to look across at me.

When the consideration hovered on the moment of inspection and awareness of a person, it was pretty much difficult to take the whole seriousness of the situation in your stride. Danielle was standing in a very elegant long bluonic flame colored dress that caught my eye.

'It is almost time for the celebrations to begin, Ensort, shall I prepare The Chamber?' Mr. Lyle spoke up in a tone that had me think of something very grey and painful.

'**The Chamber!**' I exclaimed, 'That sounds awfully like a run with the Devil, Ensort Cruvier!'

For just a moment Cruvier stared at me with a fixed smile, it was weird. He had this look of a madman, and I'd met my own fair share of them in my time.

'**How strange!** Normally we have our guests admire the image that they see as pleasurable, or at the very least satisfying to their needs. Take Danielle here, she is short, slim, pert and, if I may speak from a Gentleman's POV, she is also very beautiful. The Chamber for such a spunky young woman such as her would bring a vestage so defined she would find nothing but ecstasy and satisfaction. As of you, Lucas, I am sure with who you are, and what you are, the search for pleasure and satisfaction would not be found in The Chamber, but in some star struck woman's bed. Am I right?'

He was a jumped up prick with an ego so big, that even his clothes oozed 'Untouchable'; the top shelf garbage that knew too much to be disposed of, or too smart to call it a day – that was Ensort Dominic Cruvier. I approached cautiously and courteously to the statement.

'Apologies,' I began, my first phase of besting him at his own pursuit of "Mind Games", 'as I am without a clue what The

Chamber is, I am at a loss as to an answer. Maybe you could show me this…Chamber?'

It certainly did carry some weight in the response, much to both Danielle and Mr. Lyles' complete surprise. The surprise being that I was not reprimanded or shot on the spot for my otherwise disrespectful words.

'Mention nothing of it, Lucas, the apology should be mine to give, not yours. I was getting ahead of myself, that's all, and yes, I can offer you the time inside The Chamber. There is just one thing, however, something that I must do before you cast your eyes on the marvel that has brought so much joy and delight to only a select few lives! The night is young, the players are gathering, so why don't you chaperone lovely Danielle to the bar in The Great Hall and we will meet later?'

Cruvier was planning something, and it wasn't a celebration with my name on it. I agreed, obviously, to escorting the young woman to the bar and to spending some time with her, too.

Receiving a nod from Cruvier, Danielle walked over to me and took me by the hand before she lead me to a curtain hidden door, the curtain that Mr. Lyle pulled to the side by its cord and opened the door.

'Thank you, Ensort, I look forward to seeing you soon.' I said excusing myself from his and Mr. Lyle's company.

There was a moment of utter silence; Cruvier was still in deep thought from the polite gesture, as Mr. Lyle had fallen into a state of Flux (and we all know where that leads, right?).

'Go and have fun, Lucas…you too, Danielle, everything you want or need tonight is on the House.' Cruvier replied with a rising smirk that had Danielle turn away in disgust.

Turning to face the open door that led into a small room behind The Great Hall, I gave the young woman a short gentle squeeze of the hand. Looking up at me the way that she did, I knew that there was going to be trouble attached to meeting her – I just didn't know how much.

Walking forward into the smaller room, Danielle let go of my hand and walked over to open a set of double sliding doors that allowed the loudness of The Great Hall to spill into our

place of quiet.
 'Welcome to The Opium Emporium.' She introduced me to the sights, sounds, smells and tastes of Sodom and Gomorrah incarnate; men and women wandered and roamed the Halls with hardly a worry on their minds, or clothes on their variant sized bodies! Never had I seen anything so vividly depictive of old stories, claims and tales from people from all parts of Resheen. The question, however, was a matter of the place liking me.

Midnight Blaze

Reaching the bar in under five minutes, I was talked into having a drink of Brandy by Danielle, who found herself a seat on an empty stool by the side of a semi-clothed Bartender, Raphael. My eyes were pleased with that of Danielle's attire, which pretty much left nothing to the imagination to any Red Blooded Male. Her Rochelle Nichols full length blue dress with random placed Fire Diamonds was magnificently expensive looking, most probably bought by Cruvier for the occasion. Danielle wore it well without a single flaw; the top neck-v was darker of a powder blue scorch, below this the almost transparent soft lace fabric enhanced the trevancious alluring dark brown erect nipples that were surrounded by her small petite breasts.
 'What exactly is it that you do for Ensort Cruvier, Danielle?' I asked while I could before being drowned out by the music.
 'I introduce people...Clients, like yourself to the wonders of The Opium Emporium, Libertine. I'm not a whore, if that's what you are wondering!'
I never doubted for a minute that she was without knowledge of my Borello name, nor was I expecting to be beating about the bush with hers, either. She was a live wire in the direct line of a TNT carton, the only thing was, I doubted she even knew herself how she was effecting me.
 'Tonight I am Lucas, what would you like me to call you?'

Danielle was restrained to the particular new sensation that she had never felt before, its rise in her self-awareness and that of inclination both, bringing the defenses of her nature straight up to the surface. Suddenly, inclination hit her – hard.

'This isn't a date…I'm sorry, I…!'

The music was too loud to hear all of what she said to me, though it was with it being spoken and not shouted that I enjoyed the most. I was drawn to her lips as she spoke, the radiance in her look having my eyes scan the rest of her face before finally resting them on her eyes.

'You don't have to apologize,' I shouted loud enough for her to hear me, 'is there somewhere else we can go and have some privacy? To talk a little, I mean.'

Danielle gave an amused smile that in turn gave a glow to her face, color to her cheeks and a felesh quiver to her soft plum lipstick colored lips, that on every move of her head made the glitter from the makeup sparkle under the bright lighting – she really did like to sparkle.

With a pointing finger that I tracked to a bright red door on the balcony that surrounded the entire first floor, I nodded and set out on my way up the spiral staircase by the side of the bar. It wasn't until I felt alone that I stopped and turned around to see where she had suddenly disappeared to, but she was gone. Continuing anyway, my thoughts considered the options and solution as I made my way to the door. It was now that I was met quickly by Danielle.

'What kept you?' She joked dryly.

Stepping inside she closed the door to the world outside while we found ourselves in a warm white Chill Out Room, it's ceiling draped with woven silk sheets that shaded the powerful colored lighting set up behind each sheet. The room was quiet, quaint and most probably belonging to Mr. Lyle, my actual thoughts sounding out aloud.

Danielle laughed. '***Mr. Lyle, Chill Out!*** You would have more chance of it raining a fortune across the whole town.'

Her laugh, her smile, her look that was wrong in a place like this, especially in a place like this.

'And what about Ensort Cruvier?' I asked quickly between the laughter and short sips of Brandy that was served to us both by a waiter as soon as we entered, before they left the room to leave both Danielle and me alone.

A brief silence would have indicated Danielle was thinking about the question, which was just a question in general and not one which she should have worried herself about in the slightest. Instead of a reply of any kind I received an offering of something a little bit stronger than the Brandy – Opium.

'This is the best in the House,' she informed me as she prepared the Bubbly-Pipe for my use. 'This is from the far lands of The East, a richer, more palatable tasting selection.'

Finally having made it up for me to take I handed her one of the small lengthy pipe tails, not taking "No" for an answer.

'*I can't!*' She cried standing to her feet.

'Can't, or won't?' I replied with a responsive shrug.

She looked unhappy all of a sudden. 'I can't, that's all.'

Not pushing the matter any further I sat back in my seat and began to take in the intoxicating plumes of dense grey smoke from the bubbly that had my feet tingling within moments, certainly proving that it was definitely the best in the House.

'What is it like?' She asked returning to her seat and facing me while tucking her legs underneath herself. The momentary glimpse of her panties causing a slight stir in my loins, a twitch that indicated the first phase of an erection.

I didn't know that she was referring to something much more dangerous than opium, though there was everything in the question that pointed to the illicit drug.

'What, you've never smoked opium before?' I gasped with a rise in my buzz that had me reaching out for the Brandy.

Danielle nodded. 'Clever. I meant being The Hood, silly!'

It was then that I knew she did know who I was, but all the same, I didn't know what to tell her. The life of the notorious Borello Hood was an adrenaline rush that was all of its own; the dangers that lubricated and excited the senses in knowing that any day could be my very last. It was an intense double life that very few people were knowledgeable of, until of course my late Cousin found the answer to a long standing question on my past. Maybe it was this that had her send me away five years ago to The Saunders' Institute.

'Dangerous, I guess,' I replied lazily.

The drug was beginning to creep through my system, making me see things that weren't really there in reality, but certainly present in between the driving stone I was now experiencing.

'Why don't you chill out, sit here for a while and I'll go get us something from the stores...you look so relaxed.'

The words from her lips echoed, twisted and convulsed into frequencies of sight and color bouncing around walls and furniture. The strength of the opium was taking me through a phase of many semi-conscious fields, leading me beyond the churning buzz-feed and onto a plain that neither I, nor anyone else had ever known. Danielle had left the room when first I fell into an oblivious 'Inner Mind' journey with my thoughts and emotions, but was sitting there beside me when I finally came around from my heavy intoxication.

'***Welcome back from the grave!***' She said with a smile.

It was no time for smiles, however, as I was in desperate need of something colder than Brandy and definitely more refreshing in the way that it wouldn't fuck me up any more than what I already was.

'You need water.' She whispered leaning over to the small table behind her to lift a large vase-like jug with fresh water and ice cubes in it. 'Here, sip this.'

Pouring me a glass of the tantalizing liquid into a tall glass tumbler, she handed it to me with an absented touch of my hands that made her jump back slightly. Hurriedly she pulled away and nervously put them palms down flat to her knees, the action dragging the fabric of her dress up slightly to reveal a custom made Garter that donned a concealed Switchblade. I said nothing, assumed nothing, did nothing.

'***Shit, that was a rush!***' I cried out finding my feet again.

'Like I said, it is the best in the House. I must explain why I can't...'

I put up a single finger. 'No you don't. I already know that you can't take this with me, Danielle, because your boss won't allow any of you to smoke it with customers. Am I right?'

Nodding her head she sat back in her seat, her dress that she wore, again, began to ride up into the back of the seat. The length of her legs showing a little flesh here and there, but nothing that would have openly displayed that of her modesty. And though I couldn't really say it was easy, I forced myself to look away from her frequent glances into my eyes.

'Why do you do that?' She asked moving herself forward and pointing a steady finger at my face – at my sapphire blue eyes.

It was something that sometimes I had to do when a woman approached me with that "Fuck me until the morning" look.

'You wouldn't understand…!'

'**WHY?** Because I'm a Borello girl and not one of your Rich Blood women?' She objected with strong, harsh words.

I nodded to disagree. '***Damn it, Elizabeth, why do you…!***'

The look on Danielle's face was of anger, loathing and all the other examples of having been insulted. She was quite mad.

'By Elizabeth, you mean…?'

I couldn't believe I'd said it. The moment was corsorated with the influence of a higher mental state that I could not keep from falling short of crapping out.

'Yes. I'm sorry, I shouldn't have been thinking of anyone, I apologize. I guess being who I am, doesn't change the way I have become, you know?'

Shuffling in her seat she moved closer to me, her hand finding a comfortable place upon my knee, while carefully reaching back for the bottle of Brandy that she had brought back to the room from her short absence. Refilling my glass we both took a single sip before placing our glasses down onto the table carefully.

'The people you work for, do they know you're involvement with…Elizabeth?' She asked.

They knew, but of what Danielle knew of the people I was so stupid to get involved with in the first place, I didn't know.

'What people?' I probed.

'You are so coy, aren't you? Or is it that you prefer to keep all of your cards close to your chest?'

'And you, Courtesan, of what do you keep close to your chest when you finish here and return home? Is there a man in your life? A woman, perhaps, I don't mind, we are all free spirited.'

The topic of conversation was bordering on hot zones; of the many subjects particularly selected, speaking of relationships outside the close community of blood and friends was a sure way to find out more than what you should. Awaiting some form or answer or response, I gazed down and into her cool blue eyes rasped with onlets of green trails that made their way out into the cerulean depths, the pupil's dilating wide to enlarge the expanse of her iris, until finally I began to see inside this young woman who for the better half of the evening, had made me feel strange; the looks, glances, touches and smiles. All of these were pastured in the abyss of 'Could be', while teetering on the realms of a hidden warning.

'Tell me something?' She spoke up, her eyes still upon mine.

'Anything,' I replied.

The sound of the door handle being turned and twisted several times before stopping abruptly brought me to one conclusion, that the person trying to gain entry was that of my friend, Michael, who was probably stoned out of his face so much that he knew nothing of opening doors properly.

'Why did Elizabeth leave you…I mean, you were gone and yet, she never gave up the search for you, until they buried your empty coffin in the ground. Why would someone so struck with grief reject your return here to Borello now?'

The question was a jolt – a fucking big one at that – which had me refuse to answer, just as Michael crashed through the doors and announce he had arrived before crashing to the ground.

Laughing out loudly at his state, both Danielle and I walked over to my friend and lifted him up so that we could carry him to the sofa. He was in a sorry wasted state; his face showed signs of both dried blood and vomit, his shirt stinking of deep musky red Brandy as well as pieces of food stuck to his jacket.

'Your Brother is nothing like you!' Danielle exclaimed.

'That's because we are not Brothers, as such,' I replied

making sure that he was comfortable. 'What's with all the questions?'

Danielle fell silent, bowing her head to the floor. '*I saw you!*'

Okay, so this was a whole new level of WTF, if I can be so bold as to say?

'You saw me?'

Looking up and straight into my eyes she tilted her head slightly to the left, the length of her jet black hair with metallic cosmic blue highlights falling down over her bare shoulders and into a graceful valley of ample cleavage.

'Hollow Falls, six years ago, you were with a woman who went by the name Georgina Chilvers, do you remember?'

The line of questioning was similar, but definitely not unlike that of how a Police Officer would ask. Did I remember her, of course I did, Georgina was one of my Muses, until that day she decided to go AWOL.

Danielle stood adamant of an answer coming from me very soon, whether this was some "Break-Point" between us both, I was prepared to see it through until the end.

'Georgina Chilvers! As in Maggie and Ray Chilvers? Do you mean that Georgina Chilvers?'

Danielle nodded her confirmation. 'She never returned from her weekend break in Hollow Falls…she was my Sister, the only person and thing that I had left in the whole world.'

Moving closer I began to stroke at her arm over the smooth thin dress that clung tight to a well-toned bicep, until finally taking her hand I pulled her into me for comfort.

'I am so sorry for your loss. I can only imagine…'

'*I saw you with my Sister!*'

I was overcome with a feeling of immensely calmed anger, not at Danielle, but at the fact I was with Georgina that night she disappeared, but only three people knew this and Danielle was not one of them. That evening when The Shift opened and had both Chance and me return to Resheen, it was a memory that I would have rather forgotten.

'I seem to be feeling a little…!'

'*Fucked!*' She snapped. 'All I need to know is where my

Sister is, because you see, Lucas, all of this here doesn't mean shit to me. You are the reason I'm here.'

It was funny. My whole journey through the quandaries of my Borello life had brought me face to face with so many close calls of death, none of them even close to breaking me from the feel good and invincible belief that I lived for. The whole business with Georgina, however, was the one thing that would certainly cut a fragment of bone from my chest.

'I don't know whether to be flattered or threatened, Miss...?' Danielle made her move, quickly and swiftly, taking a switch-blade from down the side of her knee-high leatheral boot that was hidden by the dress and then put it to my throat. Something I saw in her eyes told me that she wanted to use that knife, but would a confession help save me from the titanium gilded sharpened blade?

'La Grande, Danielle La Grande.' She answered in a tone that me know then exactly who she was. 'You and that man from The Island...'

'*Man from The Island!*' I gasped.

Her hand applied pressure immediately to the blade, it's razor sharp edge nicking my skin, cutting it slightly within the feeling of an irritating paper cut that brought a stinging sensation.

'The night my Sister disappeared, you and a man from The Island met her on the cliffs of Hollow Falls. It was raining so heavy, Georgina was only supposed to be gone a short while, but for some reason she was...taken – by the man you were protecting.'

The whole turn of events began to fill my mind's eye; it was a Cyclone Storm that had been brought in from the East by a Class 6 Jetstream Monsoon, the whole area surrounding Hollow Falls was hit hard and rendering it dangerously slippery, and cold. The man that Danielle referred to was an old associate of mine from The Seacliffe and Redstone Sub-Divisional Police HQ that investigated Cold Cases, such as The Haunting of the Dog and The Bluebell Wood Mystery. Marcus Chance was a police officer who had been gifted – afflicted as he chose to call it – with the ability to disappear, but as for

Georgina, her vanishing was much more planned than even her Sister, Chance or myself could have known.

'Detective Marcus Chance was returning…Georgina was in the wrong place at the wrong time, that's all…'

Again, I felt the cold steel press against my throat. I could feel the tension, the tremble so slight within her grasp, but there was something else that I could neither fathom or figure out to be sure of her Game Plan.

'This Marcus Chance, he killed my Sister!'

I nodded to the point of realizing that any sudden moves and the blade would cut my throat, slice the jugular vein and kill me with the bleed out without a doubt.

'Nobody killed your Sister, Danielle, she was…I can't really say!' I answered with tact thrown to the wind. 'Your Sister is on The Island, I don't know where, but that is where she is.'

The response was taken hard, if only by a measure of a cooked up story that nobody else would believe. Somehow, however, I had the sense that she did with the removing of the knife.

'The Rift, it came and took her, didn't it?' She said dreamily.

'The Rift opened and she went through it, that's all I know, so the chances are she is still alive…only not here in Resheen. Now, are you going to stab me to death with the switch-blade, or are you going to tell me how the hell you know about that night in Hollow Falls?' I demanded in a low, but firm voice that had her sit back in her seat before retracting the blade and returning it back inside her boot. The way in which she did this was considered somewhat of a tease; the slow high hitch of her dress that displayed her bare skinned thigh and crotch that was covered with a pair of thin black sheer see thru panties, as her slim small hand gripped the end of the weapon and returned it slowly back into the black Leatheral sheathe.

'I was at The Valkyrie that night waiting for her, but when she failed to turn up I went looking for her myself. There was no one particular place that I would find her, I knew that, she was not far away, but far enough for me not to save her. The road from Redstone and Briarstone had been heavily flooded and there didn't seem to be any other way to get across the Hollow

Falls Flats, except take the Hill Climber. As I was taken up in the cart, I saw you, then Georgia, until seeing the man you call Marcus Chance. I only looked away for a second – and she was gone, along with your friend.' Danielle told me everything about that night, even a couple of things that I didn't know.

Standing up from my seat and walking around to the mini-bar, I fixed us both a Brandy before handing it over to her and sitting back down in my seat. She thanked me with a short strained smile that had not the slightest hint of malice or wrong doing.

'That night The Rift opened, it was your Sister who was so surprised to see us emerge from its bright intense light. She was stood in a majestic beam of radiance and utter Majesty as the rip in Resheen suddenly sealed itself shut. At the time I had no idea your Sister was going to do what she did, but the way I see it, she was heading that way anyway, well before she entered The Rift to The Isle of Storm.'

It had been an accident, clearly a case of wandering into the unknown and coming out just as confused, which she would have been once completing her journey onto the other side.

Danielle asked me if I'd been to The Island – The Isle of Storm - Storm Island to which I nodded with a look of dread.

'The Island is no place for people like us, Danielle, it's a place that has so many secrets, so many mysteries and even worse in the shape of Creatic's and Volsendekker's. If you're planning on going over there, to save your Sister, I'd step back and smell the damned coffee, because the very last place you want to be right now is on that island.' I informed her, while at the same time building up the opium bowl with the sticky tar-like substance, before taking hold of the lighter to burn the drug into a dense grey smoke that would see me comfortable in its intoxication.

My warning was taken into consideration, as was everything that I had told her that night, which was more to the point of one Courtesan Danielle La Grande suddenly disappearing from The Opium Emporium never to return again.

Queen Of Diamonds - ♦

The evening was superficially uncomfortable, especially for me, Danielle had left just before Michael awoke from his least surprising stupor and overindulgence. Ensort Cruvier did give me the information that "The Circle" had sent me to retrieve, although their failure to inform me of Danielle would cost them dearly for the fact that she could have well ended my life that very night.

'This woman, what did she look like?' The sound of a man questioned out loud, suddenly appearing from behind me, as if coming from out of nowhere.

The description that my mind was picturing at that moment in time had me trying hard to focus on the question – as well as its answer, too.

'Five-two, slim…I think she was…!'

I couldn't do this, I knew that they would have her hunted down as soon as I left that building and I didn't want that.

'Ensort Cruvier tells us that she used the name Danielle as entry to The Opium Emporium, what say you of her last name, Lucas?' The same voice shouted up more demandingly.

They didn't know who she was! I mean, yes, they knew she was Courtesan Danielle, but by no other name.

I nodded blindly deceiving them. 'I…I don't know!'

The thought that they would be unhappy with the answer didn't bother me, though having the 'Penalty of Death' lifted from my head pretty much mattered more than a minor sin of withholding the truth from them.

'*Find her and kill her!*'

At first, I was sure that the man's voice was in some way being a little angry, maybe, and that the overreaction would subside.

'I'm sorry, what did you say?' I asked after a too lengthy pause of the subsiding anger being taken back.

Again, he told me the very same thing: Kill the Courtesan.

Before leaving the building I was greeted by a rather well built man dressed in a long black hooded robe holding a briefcase, his silence telling me that he had had his tongue removed so as not to speak of any secrets.

'I don't have any need for money...'

'The briefcase contains everything that you will need to rid our town of this Courtesan, as you can appreciate, insulting you as Libertine Hood is more than a valid reason to take her head, she deserves nothing less than a quick death. Stand your ground. Become a reflection of your own potential and we will remove the Mark from your name.' The voice called to me from the darkened shadows in the room.

Taking a hold of the briefcase I started off on my way out of the building and finally into the streets where thousands of people rushed to a nearby building that was on fire across the way, my very own curiosity getting the better of me to go and see what was going on that would attract so many people.

'What is it? What is everyone looking at over there?' I shouted stopping a young man to ask him where everyone was going.

'*It's The Spire!*' He said breaking away from my grip.

Looking across and up into the dense layers of residences, I finally caught sight of The Spire; it looked shocked, fired and very much damaged by several grenade detonations.

'**What the fu…!**' I suddenly remembered. '*Blaze!*'

Leaving the crowd I made my way to The Bastion Tavern to find out if Molly Winters, the Landlady, knew of the woman who had bravely put a knife to my throat – my knowing of her being one of the rivals in The Borello Vigilante ascendants being far from my mind.

'Danielle La Grande, you say?' Molly sighed pulling me a stein of ale from The Borello House Cask. 'Why would she put a blade to your throat?'

Molly was not without knowledge, some of it vast and valuable of all her customers and those town folk who crossed her path. Her whole establishment had been built on the foundations of "Knowledge", which in the traditional values of Borello, had gained her the upper hand in many of the more important people's decisions, even with the added pressure of persuasion, too.

'Do you remember Chance, the Copper from…'

'**The Rift!** Yes, I am aware of him and his curse, too, Lucas, but why would you be involved with him?' She cried interrupting me with a strut that took her over to the Channing & Co. Cash Register that rang out its sale and ejected it's solid drawer into her well-toned stomach.

There were so many differences in my life, with Evermore being the spoken home of my settlement and Borello, the night shadow they referred to as The Borello Hood; the wanted villain who chased ghosts and bitter memories.

'Have you ever been through The Rift, Molly?' I asked, suddenly receiving a very displeased frown from her face.

Though she was angry that I didn't answer her question, Molly chose to answer mine anyway, shocking me with her reply.

'I'll tell you this, Lucas, The Rift is no place for the likes of us, you see? Resheen is our home, to do what we do, to live as we do and in some way evolve as we do…but not by using or going through The Rift. I went through that thing once and I counted the days until I returned here, it was unresheenian to say the least. Your visit there was probably more eventful than mine…'

I stopped her with a quick laugh that had me roll up my shirt sleeve to show her a long scar intracted a low swell of sliced skin that merged into my arm. 'I got this in The Estates, some kid with a knife jumped me.'

Molly was shocked, by both the scar and the story.

'A notable scar, Lucas, one that I hope you restrained yourself from any wrong-doing to the kid, I mean?'

I nodded. 'It's a bloody deep scar, Molly, what do you want me to say, that I allowed him to live?'

Again, I saw the shocked look on her face, only this time it had clear traces of disappointment; not that sanctimonious bullshit that a stranger or someone barely a friend gives, but that deep look of their regret and sparking dislike of you. Many say that this is the very same as with the creation of "Love", as well as affection between all living things. Well, according to Casanova Da Vinci anyway – who I would never doubt his clarity.

'Seriously?' She gave her 'Get out of Jail free' final chance question that would give me the option of changing the answer to an honest one. The look of hope hung freely from her and I did but oblige with a nod and sigh.

'*Of course I didn't!* The little Weasel cut me and then ran away over to the Tenements, and that's when I returned here to Resheen.' I concluded the tale and told her the truth.

Changing from doubt to a more pleasing look, maybe a little too pleasing for my liking, she poured me another stein of ale and popped it down onto the bar with a loud laugh. 'On the house, for your scar that you gained from a Scamp.'

Allowing the laughter to subside I told Molly that I needed to find the young woman, and find out as much I could about her to put to one of my sources in The Borello Police Force. At first, as you would expect, Molly was a little cautious to the mention of the law in her establishment.

'Interesting,' she said, 'Since this morning most of these in here have lost their contacts and connections in the town, so how come you still have yours then? Is there something I need to know, Lucas?'

It was then that the whole matter between Keltman and Teal finally hit me. I whispered a name under my breath, one that had Molly and several other people in the bar hush their mouths and turn to look at me.

'*Aaron Jones!* ' The initial whisper received the still of silence, to be followed by one man walking forward and asking that golden question. '***The Bastard Enforcer of Fire City!*** You know him then?'

The man I didn't know from Adam, though Aaron Jones was a different story. This different story, however, was no business of anyone's except my own.

'Hell friend, even I don't know anyone who doesn't know The Executioner, fucking Bastard Enforcer, do me a favor. This mutation of a Resheenian can cut you down at five hundred yards with a woman's Boyster Canon after a full bottle of Raven's Blood Wine.'

Everyone around the bar wooed and gasped and whistled at

the hardcore description of the new Sheriff in town, all except one, of course. Stuart Wicks. He was a man from the north who didn't give a fuck about anyone except himself. Rumor had it he ran into a rare group of Red Sheekan's and became hunted, and only for his quick thinking did he lead them onto the road of Turpin Mines. His count of seven, though believed to be an exaggeration, chased him and his Sheekal into a closed conduit that had no room for any immediate escape – but he managed to live to another day.

'Mr. Wicks, you have a look that no other man in this bar has on their face, do you wish to say something?' I shouted across the room and gained total silence. 'You served with him in The Fifty Day War, did you not?'

Molly was stunned that I knew this.

'That's right…Master Lucas, I did, and you didn't!'

'Steady now, Stuart, I don't need any shit to clear up today,' Molly warned him with a hard smack of her hand on the bar which made quite a few of the customers jump. 'Just answer the bloody question and let's move on.'

Stuart's reputation by rumor had proceeded him through each and every town he had found, discovered or tried to settle in. Though the Sheekan problem was no more a problem in many parts of Resheen, people still hired him to get rid of other more fierce Creatic's.

Approaching me with a look of tiredness and drunken stupor, he placed a hand on my shoulder and cackled a laugh.

'See me, Master Lucas…then you see Aaron Jones, too! He is the bastard you have all heard of, he is The Executioner of any man, beast or Sheekan Hal in this whole universe. You have to cut off the head to kill the beast, and any man who can do that then knows how to end his and my days too.' He told me while breathing his liquor stained breath right into my face and half blinding me with the spit that sprayed everywhere with his outbound words.

After he had told me what he thought I and everyone else needed know, he returned to his seat and sat back into the dark shadows before resting down for a nap, it's what he did most of the time when not out killing around Resheen.

'Have you seen Elizabeth today?' Molly asked discreetly.

'Not yet, I'm going to see her soon, why?'

Molly told me that there was a woman over in Redstone City who had requested an audience with me five days ago, saying only that she was from The Light. I was curious.

'One of those Goody Good's came around looking for you, left this card and a name…Crystal!'

The name meant nothing to me, though the message, as short and as cryptic sounding as it was, I knew exactly what it meant. The small double sided black calling card that had nothing but a singular triangle symbol on one side, and the name Crystal Lawson clearly showing in clear Garamond gold type.

'Nice looking card, I think I'll keep it.' I said popping it into my pocket. 'Where in Redstone is she, Molly?'

Molly grabbed a hold of my empty stein and started walking away. 'She's not. She's here in Borello, came in last night on the last train. You'll find her at The Boudoir Elegance that's on Victoria Street, room one-eight-seven.'

Thanking her for the drinks I left the Tavern and made my way to The Boudoir, which was only a few minute run across the rooftops away. Alas, however, my attire would not have me as swift in my stead, or as comfortable as those that made up my nightly visits previously.

Ironically, my passing through the large crowds gave me ample cover of being seen or detected by any of the Borello Guards or Police who were on a mission to bring me in – Dead or Alive. Already there were more than a thousand of Borello's authorities combing the area for my alter-ego, as well as all the other vigilante's that had appeared in the town over the past three decades. Many of them who would be now dead, or in prisons across the whole of Resheen.

The corner street leading onto the side alley into The Boudoir Elegance was bustling with visitors, tourists and undesirables who kept their heads down while passing others, as strangers rubbed shoulders with the masses and made their way up the street to the Market Square. My opportunity to slip into the alleyway came with a sudden pause that gave me relief to the fact that I would have been confronted by several well-armed and well prepared Borello Guards making their way into the same alleyway and disappearing into The Boudoir itself.

'***They're looking for your friends!*** ' A voice whispered in and around the air without any trace of the person who had said it. Like a whisper on the breeze came the voice of a woman, while hanging in the echo was the familiar sound that saw the hairs on the back of my neck stand up on end.

Quickly turning around to see where the voice came from, I was confronted by Elizabeth, looking good, but also weakened by the bullet wound she was recovering from.

'***Elizabeth!*** ' I gasped, taking a hold of her and leading her away from the crowds to a nearby disused doorway. 'You should be resting up…'

'***The Borello Blaze!*** ' She cried a low angry whisper, 'You are truly a man with a wide scope, I'll give you that, Lucas Cavendish – ***The Borello Hood!***'

I didn't understand why she was behaving like this, had I done something untoward her or to her dissatisfaction, then I would have gladly put my hand out for a wrap. But the way I saw it, I believed I was being accused of assisting the unknown vigilante in their damaging of The Spire that same morning.

'The fire at The Spire…'

'Are you so naïve, Lucas, that you are blind to the game? You are close to your end…an end that Borello's Midnight Blaze will bring you.'

Now I was confused. '***Are you fucking nuts!*** I have no idea what you're talking about, I don't know who this Midnight Blaze is, I swear!'

This finally convinced Elizabeth that I really didn't have any idea who Midnight Blaze was, nor did I look like I cared.

'Why did you come back, Lucas…why did you even go?'

Elizabeth's face was filled with mixed feelings of love and hate, both, but winning over her was compassion only.

'The Institute, it was…I was saved by Michael Slattery when I came back here to Borello, and he had me fixed up. When you killed my Cousin, I felt a great weight lift from my shoulders and my heart, too. I love you, Elizabeth, and I will do anything and everything in my power to win you back from this fucking cursed town. If it wasn't for them pulling my strings, I would head out to Redstone where they would never find me.' I answered telling her that it was time to get the hell out of there. She didn't know anything of my incarceration in The Saunders' Institute in Seacliffe, or of the many experiments that the evil Dr. Lions carried out on me while I was both conscious and not. For everyone in both Evermore and Borello, I was away in the America's doing my own thing and having fun between hard work and reflections on my life. My Cousin, it would seem got to have the last laugh after all – Elizabeth wasn't happy from the moment of revealing that of Melissa's deviant kidnapping plan.

'If I had known...!'

'You would never have seen me alive again, Dr. Lions made it perfectly clear, that if there was any attempt to escape or be broken out by any of my known associates, then I would have been executed.' I interrupted with good reason.

The long silence that followed began to burn my ears with the loss of words to bring us both out of the awkward moment.

'The Boudoir, what are they doing there?' I turned and asked, referring to the Guards going into the building mob handed.

'They're looking for someone,' was the only answer I got back before Elizabeth turned to me. 'What of Midnight Blaze?' The added question was not overlooked as an effort on her part to trick me; a confession in admitting knowing her now would only conclude Elizabeth's initial suspicions.

'What about her?' I asked taking from my inside pocket a cigarette and lighting it.

Elizabeth stood for a few moments looking, searching my eyes for something that would bring her out of the state she was in.

'Last night you spent your time with a woman, Danielle La Grande at The Opium Emporium, she asked you a question that you found painful...but all the same you answered it with the cold blade of steel at your throat. The Sister of the woman that you and Chance helped escape through The Rift, is that of the notorious Midnight Blaze, do you think?'

The way that Elizabeth informed me of her knowledge of me at The Opium Emporium the evening before made me nervous suddenly, as it would anyone, but even further she spoke of Danielle, the desperate young woman who just wanted to know where her Sister was with as little pain as she could deliver. Personally I was shocked.

'*That's not true!*' I gasped, 'Danielle La Grande is just an average Borello…'

'Assassin, Lucas, like you, like me, like all of our associates who roam the night. **It is not her Sister that she wants!**'

Elizabeth was not being totally open and honest with me.

'**Assassin!**' I gasped.

Leading me by the arm away from the doorway and through the dense crowd of shoppers and workers, we came by a store that sold tonics and herbal remedies. It was not unlike the Pharmacies that were plentiful throughout The Rift, but it was a place that I had hoped Elizabeth would never discover I had been frequenting of late. Like Michael, I too was "Chasing The Dragon" for better term of the condition, not the Tooting or injecting of heroin. The opium use had grabbed me like a leaf on the breeze, its soft and gentle beginnings now starting to feel like a hurricane around my veins.

'You're shaking like a junkie, Lucas, come on we'll go and see Douglas, he will make you some Tonic up that'll make you feel a lot better.' She whispered taking a hold of my hand to feel me shivering. But it was not the effects of the drug that made me tremble, but the presence of Elizabeth and the way in which she had me feel; emotionally scuttled by her awareness of me there and the zaprye that oozed from an almost visible charge of electricity from her to me and vice-versa.

'*I love you!*' I gasped out without thinking.

For a moment Elizabeth stood paused in making her entrance to the store, and then changing her mind she turned to me with an alluring smile that set me off with wave after wave of excitement, joy and bound hesitation in grabbing her in my arms to feel, to hug, to embrace with a soaring build of emotion that would see us both united as one. For the first time in a long time I was finally feeling happy.

'I love you, too, but it is what we both are that defines us to the point of expectation and action. You are a Libertine, Lucas, I am…!'

'***Don't you fucking dare!***' I cried out taking a hold of her and pulling her away from the store to the side. 'If you love me, you will leave with me… ***tonight!***'

Elizabeth did not fight my manhandling of her, nor did she make any sound of objection to my words.

'You came back for me… for Elizabeth, Lucas, but I am two and yet none the same, it is our way. The Circle have taught you of their traditions and ways, but they are not of mine, don't you see? I knew where you were when I found you here today, so I could say Goodbye!'

Like a lightning bolt from the ground passing through my whole body I felt weakened, as if downed by a relentless strike of Glandular Fever hitting me all at once. And all that I could see before me was a darkening veil of nothingness heading straight toward me – unconsciousness.

Knight's Pawn To Kings Bishop

For the many times that I had lost consciousness and then regained my senses, you would have thought I'd be used to it by now. Unfortunately, the experience wasn't as marvelous or glamorous as the knock-outs you see on television; the fast delivering punches that render the victim unconscious in a heartbeat, or the precision strike of a hardened foot that puts you out and down instantaneously. For what made me take a fall, I'd have much preferred combat as my Nemesis.

'***Welcome back from the grave!***' A soft voice of an old man sounded from behind me.

Leaning up onto my elbows I scanned around to find that I was inside a dim lit room, the floor was of concrete displaying the traits of a house, while the décor of ripped wallpaper across the walls told me I was still in Borello Town.

'Is there a point to that phrase at all?' I asked nursing the back of my head of some form of injury that I couldn't find.

'Do you play chess, Lord Cavendish? I'm sure that a well-educated man such as yourself does from time to time, am I right?' The man continued while turning around to face me.

He was tall, well built and smartly dressed in a new attire adapted by the church – he was a Priest. His face was just recently cleaned and shaven, while the smell of expensive After Shave emitted from his clothing to be welcomed by my nostrils before tantalizing my senses - Aramis.

The matter of "First things first" came to mind, along with the overwhelming urge to beat the old man to death – with his own arms that I would rip from the sockets of his body in tempered anger.

'Five seconds is all that I am…'

'I am Father Anthony Yogle, you are weak from your hunger, but we can cure that!' The man announced his name with a raised hand in the air that hushed me. He seemed interesting.

Sure, he had the Habit, the cross, the rosary beads and the haircut to indicate his said occupation, but there was **that** something about him that didn't seem quite right; above his right eye he had a tattooed symbol – a triangle – just like the one on the calling card left with a message at The Bastion Tavern for me by a woman calling herself Crystal.

'Father Anthony, huh, well, Father Anthony, I don't take kindly to people knocking me the fuck out without introducing themselves first. It was a bold move to say there's only one of you, don't you think?' I told him straight while glancing around discreetly to get my bearings, and to pinpoint the advantageous objects and fixtures that I may need to succeed in leaving there unscathed – or at the very least alive.

He stood as though pondering on the comment I had made to him, until all at once I, as well as he, saw the unmistakable signs of the shellandine moment our very confrontation in Hand to Hand combat began. He was fast, not faster than myself, but he was fast in his reactions, speed and strikes. Though not many hits were made to my own self, for the man standing in front of me with his hands and feet in stance to a further attack, I knew that "it was on".

Strike after strike, blow after blow, the sheer discipline of his mind was giving him energy in his work up to finally finish me on my arse. This was an Assassin the same as me, but who worked for the Church Warders to keep evil from wreaking its ugly violence throughout the land. This Priest was something else in the area of Hostine Dioclestium.

'You hesitate to hit out when you know you should. Again, face me and begin.'

'And you talk too much Old…!'

I was down, again, with the surprise outstep of the Priest that had me hitting out at nothing and stepping into nothing but the Punish Stance move that had me lose my balance.

'The trick is to breathe in before extending your lunges, breathe out on the strike. Again, reach deeper into your mind and find your place, Lord Cavendish.' He piped up for a second time of criticizing my balance, strike and discipline.

Again, I stood ready, this time observing the man who had one foot curved on the floor to the other. It was to be a Trendaia forward attack that he was going to initiate, its consequences of working said to render the opponent unconscious, instantly.

As soon as he raised his foot I engaged with a change of my forward hand, and then my foot to his now hesitant rush at my body. The difference was precise and also damning, as I had now just knocked out a Priest in what looked like his home.

As he lay there still and silent, I started to check him for some form of ID, or clues to why he would hold me hostage.

'*You're technique is all to shit, Kid!* ' A familiar voice sounded from behind me from the room door. 'It's been a long time Lucas…Far too long.'

That voice was Captain David Price, the heralded keeper of Lupo Cresto Aumento House in London, Overseer of my good Cousin Lord Xander O'Neill, as well as Piarsan to the infamous Cacciatori Svegliarsi Villa – Wolf Wake Manor.

'Even so, I could still put you down on your arse, David!' I greeted him with a very debatable and bold statement.
Walking inside the room David found himself a seat before sitting down and telling me to find my place back on the makeshift bed that I had awoken from. By the look on his face I knew that the news he was about to give wasn't to be easy for him to share.

'I see you've met Father Yogle! You're a hard man to find, Lucas,' David began, 'we looked everywhere for you, on and off the grid. That old Master of yours in Redstone…Mr. Ling, he said you were planning on leaving with a woman!'

He was well informed. 'That didn't happen. I hope you left him alive and well?'

David nodded while taking out a cigarette and lighting it.

'Relax, Mr. Ling was casual calling, he still has the restaurant by the lake. We dropped the ball, and I'm here to say sorry, Lucas. We had no idea you're Cousin was going to make the decision on sending you to The Saunders'…Anyway, we need your help in bringing the two towns together, and if you do, it will be one of the biggest victories since the fucking Tremorium War of eighteen-ninety-six! It's true, but we can't do this without you're help, Son.'

As much as I liked David, appreciated his help and admired his dedication in protecting Xander from harm, I couldn't help the small warning alarm inside my head sounding off a twitch in my hand – the twitch of caution and serious ponder.

'And who is it exactly I am helping, David?' I asked dryly.

David was looking really worried and with this worry there was probably the unsaid, untold consequences to such a quest that he had for me. 'The Sanctum of The Order has found eight of the twelve Houses who want to give their loyalty…I don't need to tell you how difficult these times are, Lucas, but if it makes you feel any the better, the houses appreciate your help and assistance. The Illuminati have…'

I shook my head and put up a hand with a mocking laugh. 'They want something that is out of their reach!'

'The Light, oh yeah, that figures, but it doesn't answer the

real question of your calling…they marked you!'
The Sanctum of The Order was a House, its power play was to rectify – to fix – the world in its quick decline of King's and Queen's, and we're not talking "Royal", but by The 12 Global Houses of power. For me, it was yet another story of how I was taken into their unorthodox jet stream of International Treason and crime encrusted decisions.

'Is this where you tell me to give up my day job David, and come over onto the winning side?' I replied in a way that made him smile with amusement.

'That's funny, Lucas, but seriously, you already know that it will be those of your nightly activities that would be more in question here, of course?'

'Yeah, I figured that out myself and I'm sorry, I am in a…'

'*Flux!* Aren't we all? Okay, well, I'll be staying at Riposo del Cavaliere in Briarstone, if you change your mind.' David spoke up while making his way to the door and pausing. 'I'm really sorry I couldn't help you, Lucas, we all are.'

Before he made his silent exit, I asked how long he was staying in Resheen, before heading back to London to join the rest of the Crony's that made up "The Establishment".

'I'm here for two days, after that…Well…Good Luck, Kid.'

And then he was gone. That night was the very last time I saw David Price, but for the familiarity's of his ghostly presence in the form of coincidental actions and words that assisted me in my tight spot escapes – but that was another story better left for another time. At present I had the misfortune of a Kick-Ass Mad Ninja Monk who probably shat Martial Arts, other than used it as a hobby or Service of Employment.

'Well,' he began shaking himself down, 'that was a lot better, Lord Cavendish, better than we expected in fact.'

'Where's Elizabeth?' I raised my voice and shouted at him.

He remained silent, but aware of my question for a few moments while clearing his head. The look on his face was of Hierarchy, and I knew myself that his negative answers would render him a Pawn in this game that someone else was playing. The only reason I knew David wasn't a player in all of this, was because I knew he was on his way to change the world to a much better place, an obvious oversight of The Bastion Tavern and my meeting with Elizabeth outside The Boudoir Elegance.

'Why does she serve you?' I demanded.

'Elizabeth Spinks does not serve us, Lord Cavendish, she serves The Light, as she has always done – as do you!'

I was pretty much detached from his statement, especially as it implied my part in something that I wasn't aware I was.

'*I serve no man!*' I cried out readying myself for combat.

'No, Lord Cavendish, you do not…you serve The Light.'

Rushing at Father Yogle I jumped into the air for a Folly Foot Press to his chest, but was taken by the ankle and pushed into the nearby wall. Not allowing the Priest to get the better of me, I got up as quickly as I could as he came running at me with his hands out straight – his thrust was met with a punch, then a kick to the stomach, chest and face. His weakened position had given me the perfect opportunity to fix him in a stance of the ultimate execution – The Death Snap.

'Who sent you?' I demanded holding him steady.

Father Yogle smiled. 'What does your heart tell you?'

I was starting to feel strange, feint maybe, but strange all the same. My thoughts were not those of my own anymore, they were oblique, strewed and unfamiliar to me; two men appeared within my visionary decline of energy, they were wearing an old form of dress, while in their midst they happened upon a light radiating intensely…then the vision faded as my strength came back to me. Father Yogle had taken advantage of the moment of weakness and escaped, both my Death Move and the room.

'*Son-of-a-Bitch!*' I screamed out looking around the room as if trying to find something to smash into pieces. I was angry. Making my way out of the room I noticed that the whole inside of the building was some unused warehouse, it was near the village of Prairie Ridge, by the river that headed north to Nasperine, while back the way was the main hub of The Chorim River that ran directly under Borello Church. It was irony flowing in the shit that lined the very town.

The Mad Monks

Silently I entered Borello Church under cover of the night and the sounds of the many drunkards that made their way down into the Subsystem, the one place that they could find peace for the long night of sobering up ahead of them. The Church was quiet, silent except for the creaks and moans of the wooded floors that brought caution and stealth a must to my continuity. Finally I reached the end of the hallway landing where upon looking down I saw both Father Yogle and Father Benedict, my overhearing of their conversation brought new information and wisdom to my ears.

'You look worried Anthony, is there something wrong?'

'Captain Price is here, in Borello, looking for Cavendish!' Yogle replied with a sadness. 'Maybe we should…!'

Father Benedict walked straight up the Priest and slapped him repeatedly three times across the face, and then with a quick turn on his heel, he ordered Father Yogle to bring him the prisoner!

While Yogle was away getting whoever it was that Benedict had referred to as a prisoner, I snook down the stairs and into a nearby alcove where I would get a better view of the entire room. And, it wasn't too long before Yogle returned with a man, or woman with a dark sack placed over their head.

'***Ah, here we are!*** Are you ready to talk?' Father Benedict asked in a goading manner that had the prisoner shake their hood covered head from side to side without a sound.

'I had always imagined this town being better than any of the others, you know, a rejuvenated place of decency and pride. Now, you were brought here for a reason, do you remember what that reason is?'

Benedict was relishing the time torturing the poor bastard that it seemed they were under the power of the two Priests. Father Yogle turned to face them when they didn't answer quick enough, striking out a hand and knocking them half way to the ground, before they steadied and straightened up again.

'It matters not that they do not speak Father Yogle, if only they listen and understand what they have to do.' Benedict was somehow protective of the prisoner, but why? 'Bring me the sword of the Outlaw Deadly Night Shade, and you will be free from our service, do you understand?'

This was somehow all messed up! Shade…Elizabeth had been captured along with me in the streets of Borello, the drug which had been used on me would have to have to have been used on her too, unless…!

'We have a bonus job for you, too, kill her and The Borello Hood by Midnight tonight and you will be rewarded with a safe passage to Nasperine. Fail, however, and you will be the one being hunted by Dawns early light.'

Taking the prisoner forcefully by the arm, Father Yogle took them from the room, just as I made the decision to make myself visible.

'Make a fucking sound and I'll kill you where you stand, do you understand?' I called out to Benedict in a quiet voice, a voice that had the Priest reach for his sword under his Habit.

With a slow wave of my finger I patted the left breast of my jacket. The "Dare to try me" look on my face, begging him to reconsider his intentions.

'Your steel will mean nothing to my lead, Father, so do us both a favor and throw down your weapons.' I warned while a moment later he slowly disarmed himself and threw the sword down by my feet, which I quickly picked up and walked over to him with the blade focused on his chest.

He wasn't happy with the bluff – It was a bluff worthy of an applause – but the Priest decided to smile mischievously at the way I had successfully tricked him.

'**You're here for the girl!**' He exclaimed turning around and pointing at his overfilled desk of papers and documents. 'If I told you that you were…!'

I gave him no time to speak out his arrogance and lies or taunts any more, as with a quick lunge with the sword he once owned, I drew him through the chest and straight through the heart. It took but a few seconds of him trying desperately to speak, but eventually Father Benedict gasped his last and fell to the floor dead. His blood was rich and deep red in color, the travin's were long and wide by the time Father Yogle came back and entered the room filled with emotion at seeing his friend and dear colleague dead at my feet.

'Surrender your weapons, Father Yogle, or you're next!'

My surprise at his reaction came with an immediate force of stance and readiness, while in the time that followed, no one man between us had come to face a life altering situation as the one we were now in; his Paroxinate now dead, Father Yogle had only anger, vengeance and death on his mind – my death.

'You taint our walls with blasphemy, you kill in cold blood one of our Brothers, and then demand I give up the only thing that stands between The Darkness and The Light! All I hope, is that you were paying attention, Lord Cavendish!'

For near-on forty-five minutes the Priest and I fought it out in the traditional Hand-to-Hand Combat, occasionally picking up chairs, oddments and large fittings to encourage a quicker end. Finally, I had wounded him, as he had me, but the wound was far from fatal, or of importance to me. As for Father Yogle, the flesh around his wound was open wide enough for the flesh to flap about while he punched, kicked and rushed at me with all he had left to give.

Broken and bruised skin, chipped and broken bones, teeth and blood abound spattered, strew and fell in all directions coming from nowhere and scattering everywhere. Finally, he tired.

'You know…Cavendish, you were always The Knight's Pawn, even when you are dressed up in that Clown outfit you call the perfect disguise. We own you…you serve The Light…you serve us…'

And again, as with Father Benedict, I performed the last fatal finishing move that ended another life in less than an hour. My only conviction of this drastic measure being their attempts to kill me, though the law, the people of Borello and my dear Elizabeth, would not have believed the story.

'Bravo, Libertine, you **are** indeed as good…if not better than they say back in Florence. Two Paroxinate Priests from The

Light in one day...'

I turned to face the voice that belonged to a familiar young woman I had become briefly familiar with, her standing up in the eaves and gables of the Church hiding her until she jumped down onto the hard dry wooden boards near Father Yogle.

Danielle stood before me, her luminescent cosmic blue hair just visible under the black cloaked hood that hid for a few moments the slim tight fitting Leatheral's, thin white silk shirt and almost exoset pair of black knee length boots. The only thing that she was missing that night was a mask of disguise, though I very much doubted she was banking on allowing anyone to know who she really was, especially me. From inside her cloak she took a switch-blade, its shiny pearlescent blue handle catching the moonlight as she flicked her wrist and released it with precision at my chest.

'**YOU...!**' I gasped catching the knife's blade between the two quick reflexed palms of my hands. 'Shouldn't be playing with knives!'

Danielle was surprised by the reaction, one which brought her to taking out an identical second switch-blade that she held in her hand tightly.

'Impressive,' she complimented with a bow that released the second blade and directed it not at me, but at the bow rope by my side. It was a distraction; My looking away from her to pinpoint the knife would give a perfect opportune moment in which to render her final sneak attack upon me; weaken, maim, disfigure, even kill me.

The boiling blood in my body shot through every vein, every fiber of my being to generate surging adrenaline that had given me the strength, speed and power to deal with the two deadly assassin's. It was with a raised sword in my hand that came to end Danielle's attack. The shortened cold steel blade pierced her stomach, gravelling through the skin with a sludgy squelch that emitted the blood which changed the white blouse into a crimson red stain. Taking a hold of her the best I could from the impalement I rested her down onto the floor gently.

Looking into her eyes for what could have been the last time, I could see the pain, anguish and clasping effort she made to make the journey into death less painful than it already was.

'Who are The Light, Danielle?'

'You…are…too late! The Church will come after…you…!'

Danielle lost consciousness. My quick actions had caused a psychotropic Flux in my reactions of bettering the situation, so much so that I picked her silent still body up from the floor and rushed her as fast as I could to the nearest back street Doctor I knew, who just happened to be a friend of Michael Slattery-Gruber's.

'**She needs help, she was drew thru with a sword…this sword!**' I gasped as soon as Doctor Harper opened her door and allowed me to hurry inside to place Danielle on the sofa.

'This is quite unorthodox, Lucas, she's…'

'Save her, please, Doctor Harper!' I begged her.

It was right what she was saying, it was not the way that she operated her "After Hours" private surgery, but I had no other choice but to take her there.

'Alright, get me some clean water, towels and the bottle of Scotch from on top of the kitchen table.' She finally conceded and began giving me instructions to help.

Taking a hold of her medical bag, Doctor Harper brought out a pair of surgical scissors that she used to cut through the tight material that made up Danielle's once bright white blouse. The wet bloody fabric was sliced quickly in an upward direction until it was pushed to one side. The entry wound of the blade had cut her a couple of inches away from her naval, while the loss of blood had stained her entire stomach, chest and small perk breasts. Looking down at her being tended by the Doctor, I could not help but notice her bare breasts – they were beautiful; scattering of pale skin set off the purge of darkened brown areolas where stood two hardened pointed nipples. Yes, each were bleached in blood from the wound, but they were almost alluring to my eyes.

'How long has she been unconscious, Lucas?' Harper asked.

'A few minutes, seven at the most.' I replied as the Doctor now threw her ear down to Danielle's chest to listen to her

heart. 'Will she be okay?'
Starting CPR the Doctor nodded her head with no best answer before asking me to leave and wait for her call, something that at first I didn't want to do – I wanted to stay.
Pulling me to one side forcefully, she ordered me to listen.

'This woman has lost a lot of blood, she is having problems with her heart and, I don't think you would want to be caught here with a dead woman's body to add to the other charges and misdemeanors, do you?' She said making perfect sense.

'Okay, but you will contact me as soon as there's news?'
Harper nodded with a reassuring smile that gave me every bit of confidence that Danielle was going to pull through – and why wouldn't she pull through? Dr. Harper had brought me back from the brink of death, so why not Danielle?
Leaving the lavish home on Muir Road that was on the far western side of town, just five minutes from The Borello Church and Bell Tower, I headed back into town to The Bastion Tavern.

'***What the hell are you doing here, Lucas, the whole Guard are out looking for you!***' Molly cried out as soon as I entered.

'They're always looking for people like me, Molly…'
'This is different,' she said with a worried voice taking me by the hand and leading me around the back of the bar and through into her own private quarters at the rear of the Tavern. The rooms were immaculately clean and nothing like the old tattered and used public bar that catered for the drinkers, the drunks, the loose women and regular haunting punters.

'Nice place you have.' I quipped walking up to a mantel and picking up a picture that had both Molly and a well-dressed man standing together for a pose in front of Redstone Falls.

'I keep it the best I can…that's Jed Mills, he's the…'
'Devil's Crown Champion Racer!' I interrupted with a look of amazement. 'Five consecutive wins through eight seasons, one all-time defeat of Harry Stena and Jordan Lascelles.'
Molly was certainly surprised by my interruption.

'I wouldn't have put you down as a racing person, not of the

vehicle kind, anyway. Did you ever meet him?' She replied in a strange tone, as if fishing for something.
I fell into my thoughts for a moment. 'I think we met during his second race against The Specter – James Grant Junior.'
Molly responded to the name as if someone with an axe to grind would, but a lot less the attitude of a woman on a mission or enraged with misfortune. Molly was saddened.

'He was a great driver, one of the best on the circuit during the eighties, until Jackson arrived and corrupted the whole thing. That is the man who killed him, June fifth, nineteen-eighty-four…'
My reaction at the news halted her with a sudden jolt.

'Eighty-four! Are you sure…I mean, I was there in eighty-four when he raced Edmondson, Muir and Simpson.' I informed her with the utmost surety.
For this information being repeated, most probably for the umpteenth time, Molly shook her head vigorously in objection.

'Jed Mills was killed after racing Ralph Henson on the sixty-six, the unofficial race that Jackson organized and fixed. He never knew of mine and Jed's relationship, something that will see the end to his life, as he ended my…!' She stopped with a glance around as if to try and take back the hint of words.

'**Husband!**' I whispered finishing the sentence for her.
Molly nodded with an unease of me knowing this, before she made her way over to a wall cupboard and attempted to take from it a large black square box that I lent a hand pulling out so she could access it. Inside were clothes, medals of war, odds and ends that both Jed and Molly had collected over the years, but more notable than these items was that of his old Borello Army Uniform; its clean silver buttons perfectly placed around a well-kept clean jacket and trousers bearing the insignia's of the B.F.A's logo pins and patches that had been sewn on perfectly.
It was strange how the little things in our lives made the most of our emotions, as was the case of the old worn clothes and memories that were sat in front of us. Molly took from the box a Torso Utility Belt, it's strappings still strong and new looking,

while down the several connected interlinks sat a Briacco short sword, two Vieger six shot pistols and plenty of reserve ammunition. These were among the best in weaponry from The Borello Army, besting those of Evermore slightly by their ease of use and fatality.

'Take these.' She said without hesitation. 'These will help you in your darkest days, Lucas, take them with my blessing and the blessing of my husband. Maybe with these in your hands it will deal justice to the likes of Warren Jackson, who will never feel the Karma of his sin, but those who are like The Jackal, who will feel the pain of their shame by your hand.'

I understood what she was telling me; one man's vengeance can still be found in the heart of another, and so justify the means in which to find absolution and peace.

Looking down at the uniform I noticed something odd about the ident which was of neither Borello, nor Evermore, it was marked with the symbol of a triangle, while inside there were two Sheekan's in a death grip.

'That insignia...'

Molly slammed shut the box as if angry of my enquiry.

'Tell me something...I mean, really tell me something that separates you from The Light, Lucas?' She asked.

There was no point in disputing the fact that I was aware of The Light, my involvement unknown as to how deep I had been placed within their web. The truth was that The Illuminati was here, in Borello, in Evermore, too, as well as everywhere else in the whole of Resheen. The simplicity of the tale being my way of Independence and freedom, as there's was to traverse the Common Rights of each man, woman and child and shape a world in an impetuous balance of greed in power.

'**The Circle!**' I replied without shame.

Molly was not surprised by my answer, nor was she knocked from her train of thought in delivering the reason in asking me the question in the first place.

The Circle was Borello's very own ancestral legacy; a five hundred year old Secret Order with the strength of any other in the outer world of Resheen, and within the whole tainted soils that made up the lost lands. Its members unknown, unlabeled and without identification of one another, except in very rare and special circumstances.

'The Light finally meets The Darkness!' Molly gasped.

'I am but a simple Libertine, Madame Molly…'

'*NO!*' She exclaimed grabbing the Leatheral straps from my hands and shaking them before me. 'You are the two bound by one, vested by Faith and driven by The Light. You are the Lord of the night, the bringer of justice and truth, but not the one who will bring Borello to the sound of Freedom. Take the weapons and go, Lord Lucas Cavendish of Evermore, and may god go with you on your journey.'

Taking the straps and making my way out through the living quarters back into the bar, I gave a last look back at Molly, who had followed behind me to wait. Her face showed a look of hope, as well as having the smile of pride upon her face.

Making my exit from The Bastion Tavern I looked up and out across the town to see the many shops, houses, wood beam rooftops and cobblestone streets that led the way to a darkened shadow caused by The Borello Bell Tower – it stared back at me with a taunt that only I was familiar with; a time so long ago in the past when the only friend I had was the night, and the learning curve of necessity and violent lessons that brought those odd and sometimes scary repercussions of a much darker side to my alter-ego.

Check Mate

The journey back to Michael's Borello Apartment was quick and pretty easy as I'd used the known hidden shortcuts of the old town, more so for the fact I knew most, if not all those of The Subsystem. When I arrived at the door there was a letter stuck to the glass – handwritten with a signature:

Vigilante Hood,

We know your true identity and the people who have protected you, but no longer. The Sympathizer known to you as Michael James Slattery is in our custody and will, if you do not adhere to an immediate surrender of yourself to the Borello authorities, be put to death by firing squad. Your move.

Enforcer Aaron Jones

If I said that it was bad news, it would be an understatement; as Aaron Jones had already established a Bastard reputation in over seven major cities and towns throughout Resheen. His ways were of torture, humiliation, battery and even murder.
Tearing the scribbled letter from the window I checked up and down the lengthy corridor to make sure nobody had seen me return to the apartment before slipping quickly inside and securing the door behind me. With haste I rushed to the bedroom and ridded myself of my clothes while dressing in a much comfortable attire; the black and silver seamed softened silk shirt, black Leatheral pants, Osky Boots and Deshlan & Bloche interwoven full length jacket with matching black dragon cured hood that gave me perfect stealth in the dark. Along with the weapons' straps and prefixed long quarter sword I was ready to leave, to accept the invitation of this Enforcer that was now becoming a thorn in my side – an itch that had to be scratched and ridded of irritation and threat of

infection.

Making my way out through the rear of the apartment and up onto the rooftop, I took in the smells, listened to the sounds and marveled at the sights of Borello from as far up as a few hundred feet. The welcome back to "The Game" was given by several of the unknown spectators who I bumped into whilst working my way through dense steam conduits and over the wide gaps that lay hidden from one building to the next. Eventually, I had made it to Borello Police Station − it looked quiet, still and empty of all officers. Even the doorway leading up to the small reception desk looked deserted. It was far too quiet for this time of day.

'*It's a trap! They want you to go inside!*' Elizabeth's voice spoke up almost silently behind me.

'Have you come to finish the job, Shade?'

My question − my tone − was off slightly, enough to let her know that I knew of her service and the service in which was allowed to her by The Light.

'You're already dead, you just don't know it yet!' She replied quite dryly. 'The other woman, Danielle La Grande, too, as of all of us here in Borello. Darker days are upon us all, Lucas.'

Maybe there was something that she knew that I didn't.

I didn't understand. A much closer look at Elizabeth had me gasp with despair; her skin was grey-looking, eyes sunken to a point of showing black rings around the lashes as well as the way that she walked with paused thought as to where her next step was going to be.

'*The wound!*' I gasped.

Elizabeth looked down before pulling away the top of her blouse and revealing my worst fear − she had been fatally hit; that which they called the 'Slow Departure', where a wound so deep, so damaging and without a doubt lethal would begin a slow death.

'*Fuck! Fuck! Fuck!*' I snapped out loudly.

Elizabeth made her way over to me and rested a gentle hand on my face. 'That's a lot of "Fucks" Lucas…'

Without thinking, without as much as a pause, I took a hold of

Elizabeth by her waist, pulling her close to me and kissing her passionately on the lips. As I probed my tongue around the inside of her mouth I began to feel a response – a twitch at first, then followed by a return hug, cuddle and need to be kissed. There we were in a lovers embrace, whilst down in the street below outside the police station several officers arrived in an unmarked van.

'You pick your moments, Lucas!' I heard Elizabeth gasp as all at once she pulled me away from the edge and out of sight of the officers.

'What is this?' I asked quietly referring to the way in which we were still embraced with a need in both of us to take it further. Elizabeth looked deep into my eyes with a travaxus expression.

'If we live, we leave together and live Happily Ever After.'

'And if we don't?' I asked releasing my hold of her.

'Then we still leave together, just not into the sunset.'

It was a stupid question, though not a jinx-filled taint that would place bad luck at our feet, but a stupid question all the same that had the return answer not so stupid as to laugh.

'Tonight we change Borello. Are you ready?' I sighed while making sure she was ready to enter the police station with me.

Just then there was a sound behind us, nothing as to indicate a person as such, though the slight odor, smell in the air that brushed against my face was of a familiar perfume – Blaze!

'We have company!' I whispered to Elizabeth taking out my Vieger 6-Shot from its holster and hung it down by my side out of sight.

From the rooftops I saw nothing but the blacked out edges of the shadows that brought each and every building to the very tipping point of the bright Moonlight above us, and with the unnaturally warm breeze of an unexplained hot weather rise the sweat from my overheated head ran down into my eyes.

'I can't see anything…!'

Just then a figure, the same figure as I had seen earlier from the woman I'd ran through with my sword suddenly appeared. To say she had been kissed by my blade, Danielle La Grande was looking pretty well – alive even!

'Don't for one minute take my decision to save your life as weakness, Blaze! Come forward slowly and yield.' I shouted out to her reactless stance.

Elizabeth asked me if she was somehow hard of hearing, until finally the assassin made her way down to where we stood, her weapons sheathed and a look of restraint on her face.

'I yield to no man...or woman. Hello, I see you have recovered from your battle with the Enforcer's, Elizabeth!' She spoke in a "matter of fact" tone.

Elizabeth bit to the baiting tease, but stopped herself from going for the gun that was spread across her waist to prepare it to fire at the young woman.

'Good choice!' Blaze whispered with a disrespectful laugh. 'I would hate to shoot you with your own gun!'

It was time to call this "War of Psychology" off before one, or all of us ended up locked in combat against ourselves, and not the real enemy of our hour – The Enforcers – Aaron Jones.

'Unless you two are going to get down and get fucking dirty with one another, I would strongly suggest we all calm the fuck down and come to some form of agreement.' I blasted moving forward and bringing my gun up into the air to point directly at Blaze's head.

Elizabeth took the thought of the option I gave with a little less 'Crème de la Crème' than what Danielle did, as Danielle gave a sign that she was actually considering the obnoxious statement that had Elizabeth thump me hard in my ribs.

'What are you doing here?' I asked Danielle, lowering my gun and putting it away back into its holster.

Though the situation was strange; both women had some form of interest in me, even if one of them wished to see me dead. I couldn't help but wonder what had happened to Dr. Harper.

'You lied to me about Chance, Lucas, you lied about it all!' She cried out in a damning tone that should have really had me taking her over my knee and spanking her.

Elizabeth knew nothing of Danielle and I's connection in this whole affair, which brought the score to one-all; Danielle's mad crazed hunting down of Shade had been initiated before

The Borello Monks charged her with the task – but by who?

'Tell me of The Borello Monks, Danielle, who pulls their strings from behind the scenes?' I counter forced my demand over her accusation of fabricating the truth of her Sister's strange disappearance.

It was a face-off of nerve, confidence – Dominance – that had her submit to answering the question. Elizabeth was also on her pins as to preparing to draw her sword, prep her Prusant .48 weapon or set a stance to fight.

'You already know the answer to that, Lucas, all of you Rich Bloods know the answer…!'

'You're Sister is in Spirin, she's on The Island!'

The whole tension in the air was felt by all three of us at the exact same time, the prospering climax of closure enriching the night air as it made its way around us.

Danielle drew her knives from under her hooded cloak, throwing them down to the asphalt roof floor before looking up and into my eyes with a lost stare that began searching the chasms of my very soul. As soon as our eyes met, I was hit with an immeasurable force of Tremadale – I was Fluxed!

'I have searched every city, every town and every village in and around Resheen…I couldn't…I was…!'

Something strange that instant happened as soon as she had "found" what she had been looking for since the moment we both first met at The Opium Emporium as strangers, and it was strong enough to render Danielle unconscious; falling but not hitting the ground as I caught her light fragile body, it was in the brief seconds before her standing consciousness, I saw both her eyes become like a Cerulean Sunset; deep bright massing swirls of luminescent blue trail amplet's that weaved their way from the pupil into the sea blue crevices bleached with green riveral routes, to finally come replaced with the most beautiful spectacle I had ever seen.

'**Sniper!** ' Elizabeth gasped, her claim being of suggestion rather than fact of the three of us being under attack.

I held out an outstretched hand to stop Elizabeth making any reaction to the thought, steadying Danielle in one arm and lowering her to the floor.

'No, not a Sniper, she's feinted.' I assured her there was no immediate present danger. 'She saw something that changed her...changed her eyes somehow!'

It was an incident that would not have been believed unless those questioning the act had seen it first-hand themselves, though handicapped with the inevitable bonding of love, it would be Elizabeth for one who would not put into doubt my claim. Moving me out of the way she knelt down by Danielle's side and took a hold of her cooling hands.

'She needs rest.' Elizabeth piped up all of a sudden. 'Rest and medicine to keep her alive.'

Something inside me snapped. '***No!*** No medication, she'll be fine...she just needs plenty of air.'

I was out of character at the fact that I was beginning to see a phased shimmer covering the whole of the Moon, it's strange translucent texture making it unbelonging to the night sky in every way possible. Was it that of a Haze Burst from a setting Midnight Sun somewhere else in Resheen?

'***She's going cold!***' Elizabeth exclaimed.

'***She'll be fine!***' I yelled back at her, my eyes setting off some majesty of transformation, just as Danielle's had when she became tremistically emotional to the point of passing out. For me, however, the surge that beckoned my unconscious did not have the reserve will of anger, hate or intentions as those that Danielle had to fight with.

'What the fuck is...happening to me?'

Feeling the effects of whatever it was that had now made me weakly fade off slightly, I rushed to Danielle and brushed her cheek with a soft, gentle hand that felt the warmth returning to her body, the color returning back to her cheeks and a slight reveral movement of her head as slowly she opened her eyes to look around at both Elizabeth and me. At first she saw Shade, her face filled with a concern at the fact that she was still lying on the ground, while upon her gaze I saw as she did the felextural incass of both our changed eyes.

'What is it?' Danielle asked, her heart beat slowing to an

almost normal rate that brought the once bluey-green eyes she had first greeted me with to return back to normal.

'I don't know…but you look fine now,' I said turning to Elizabeth for a compact mirror or any other reflective object or commodity that she and other women walked around with.

'Do I look like a fucking AVON kind of girl to you?' Elizabeth barked back, slapping my hand out of the way as she walked off toward the ledge to check the police station.

Informing me that she couldn't feel her legs, I told Danielle to relax and I would carry her somewhere that she will be safe. Lifting her from the ground I gave a low **psst**! Elizabeth looked around and bowed her head with a loud sigh.

'And what about Michael? It's twenty minutes to the deadline and we're about to walk away?'

She was right, Michael was still being held captive in the Police Station, right where the End Game Target was, too, and the only one thing to stop the beginnings of what The Houses considered to be a **"Mother of all Fuck-ups"** in regards to "Peace". But, as always, the long arm of authority kept its distance as to the truce baring Lords and Ladies that had to work this whole plan of Treaty and Honor out themselves.

'I have to make a call, but first we all get the hell out of here and get somewhere safe…***shit!***' I replied beginning on my way before stopping quickly. 'The apartment…'

'Borello Heights! We go to Borello Heights, follow me,' I was met with Elizabeth's chosen location and a head start across the roof tops as she quickly took up the weapons Danielle had thrown down before passing out.

The radials, hatches and skylines became our foot holds as we rushed forward, jumping over and scrambling onto sill, beam and boardwalk that brought us to the very epicenter of Borello and into the court yards of Borello Heights; five hundred resident's squeezed into tiny flat let's and apartments that were over-populated and should only house half the number, many complaining of sickness and disease spreading throughout the whole building structure.

'This way,' Elizabeth called pointing over to a stairwell that reached every floor from the ground upward. 'Don't worry, we'll get the elevator, if you prefer?'

Her words were refreshing, least to say welcoming from the expectation of reaching any floor while carrying Danielle, who was by this time becoming like dead weight in my arms.

Elizabeth made her way up the first set of stairs before turning and making sure that I was still following behind, and then in a paused finger moment she signaled me to stop where I was.

'Wait here.' She whispered while sneaking off to the edge of the corridor to check the way. 'Come on, quickly!'

Catching up to her we came to a door to one of the flat let's that donned faded purple color paint, peeled with weather and shabby with use. Knocking in three successions of three, two and three, we stood waiting for an answer.

'A friend?' I turned and asked Elizabeth.

'*Maybe he's my husband!*' She cussed back at me just as the door opened and introduced another young woman who had nothing on her body but an open top sheer negligée so transparent that you could make out her shapely hour glass physique. The reflective moonlight tracing through the thin material, licking lightly across her well-toned stomach, shadowing her naval and drawing with flavor the unmistakable sight of two stiff nipples around the small pink puffy areola's.

'WTF Elizabeth, you know I'm on curfew! Christ! Whose this…and why is he carrying a dead girl?' The woman blurted out hurrying us into the apartment and closing the door.

Elizabeth took control for a moment, instructing me to take Danielle through into the bedroom and put her down on the bed. Then, while I was out of the way, Elizabeth explained the best she could our situation, leaving out the violence and death for better matters left alone and unsaid.

'We need a place to stay for a couple of hours Caterina, just a couple of hours, no more. I promise.'

Caterina Mitchin was an outsider to Borello, as she came from the north, from somewhere nobody had ever heard of, let alone been. Nobody had ever been as far north of Resheen as Nasperine and come to return with any tales, but Caterina, she seemed to be a little difficult to believe she was from somewhere that wasn't local. Her face was paled with that of a permanent none-glow complexion which for me cried out vitamin deficiency, while her eyes were shallowed by a cuspvas brown scurry which radiated a much louder and more eager cry to being heard – opium addiction. For me, Caterina's quiet vice was seen as a possible liability; what would be stopping this woman from breaking to the hardened arc of the drug, and in a moment of desperation bring the heat of the authorities down on us like Christmas?

'The Borello Police have put out a report on the TV and the radio…they want you and The Borello Hood really badly. That new Enforcer, Jones, he doesn't look like the kind of person who fucks around, Elizabeth.' Caterina voiced her concerns to all three of us, more so Elizabeth who was sat pondering on something that she didn't quite like thinking about.

'The Borello Cops are clueless to where we are, if that puts your mind at rest, but I really do need to make a call.' I let the young woman know exactly where she stood before excusing myself from her presence and making my way back up the hallway into a small kitchen.

Phoning home to Evermore I talked with Mr. Frobisher, my appointed help in the matter of Lord to the Manor, who instructed me to stay where I was and not to go out into the streets. As I informed him, I was not intending going anywhere until I knew that my friend Michael was safely away from harm – especially those of The Enforcer's.

Returning back to the living room I found both Elizabeth and Caterina sat on one of the sofas tending to Danielle, their laughter taking away a heavy weight from my shoulders, as well as the three young women, too, I was sure.

'Did you make your call?' Caterina asked walking over to me as soon as she noticed that I'd returned to the room.

I nodded with a smile. 'Yes thanks, is there any chance of a coffee while we wait?'

Caterina was more than happy to play host, even while still dressed in her night wear that Danielle was starting to take a pretty good shine to.

'If you have it in a size ten, then you and me are going to be friends forever.' Danielle yelped out with hope that Caterina did have one that would fit her, too.

Unfortunately, the tenant was two sizes up, but this didn't stop the two women in my company letting their hair down a little by putting on a private fashion show of Caterina's wardrobe.

It was fun to watch them select, choose, organize and hang the individual clothing against their bodies.

Fahrenheit Opium

The styles of Anne Marie Quaid clothing from Seacliffe's Rain Piadoru outside Resheen were the latest rage in both Evermore and Borello, as well as other towns. The Stage Set and Starlight range having been considered "Risqué" by any man's measure, but still, with half a bottle of Sheekan Wine and a Mustard Pot of opium on the boil, the brief parody's by the three women slowly began to change my mind. Danielle was sat up and now able to manage a little walk around the room, while Elizabeth and Caterina teased their Camie's, Flow and Half-Cut tops that didn't seem to sit right on either of them.

We were in the deepest depths of Borello, not so far as to say that we were hidden from everyone, because everyone included the Masked Frontierer's of fundamental change. Those who had been, and were still considered to be great enemies of the Borello Town Authorities and who had also been marked for K'jen Sukio: Immediately Execution on sight. And, it was after receiving a text from the great and honorable Mr. Frobisher, telling me that Michael had been extracted from The Police Station without harm that relaxed me a little. It was now a certainty that everyone in that room I sat in while taking the smoke of the opium were now also all marked for death, too, including Caterina.

'You're quiet, Lucas!' Danielle said jumping down by the side of me and taking a tail of The Dragon etched Bubbly Pipe sitting on the low set coffee table in front of us. Watching as she took the tail between her soft quivering lips, pulling in the smoke and teasingly blowing it back out again with such ease, I began to believe that maybe her whole life was filled a little unevenly on the road, if you can understand?

For more than nine years I had sat, stood and laid by the side of so many people who had unloaded their problematic worries and woes upon me. There were those few, however, who would unintentionally verbalize their secrets; they're more than insignificant crimes, inadvertent steals, lapsed chores and even unbridled passions that lead to "Love". I had heard it all, as well as learning that curve of psychological evaluation.

'How's your wound?' I whispered avoiding an answer to the soon to be obsolete statement.

'It's good,' she answered looking me in the eyes and trying to look for something, like before, but this time different. 'Will you be trying it again?'

The seemingly normal question that came from Danielle was not as innocent or as mistaken as she would have had me believe. I was suddenly panic bound.

'**What!**' I gasped out loud. 'I only did it because you…oh, right…you're not talking about the…I'm sorry, carry on.' I got the whole thing wrong, again, and now I suddenly found myself inside a maelstrom of one kick-ass Flux; the sheer force of embarrassment clearly showing on my face to the one person who I felt strange around. My thoughts on her were neither sexual, or none sexual, they just were. I had been up against a lot of arsehole's and patriot's, but while I alone faced Danielle's alter-ego - Midnight Blaze – I knew then that she was the real deal: 60% Assassin and 40% Resheenian.

'Don't worry, forget about it, I have,' she whispered bringing herself closer to my side. 'Actually, I meant Michael's quite scary situation…'

Finishing my smoke I grabbed my cup of coffee that Caterina had recently made and sat back carefully in my seat. The power of the opium was circulating, churning the vitals and bersenken to the matter of driving my intelligence to a surface riddled with alternative meanings and stirring emotions.

'Why are you here?' I asked suddenly with a raised voice.

'You brought me here, remember?' She answered becoming a little bit cautious by the tone.

'I mean here, now, with all of us? Michael would have gone to the ends of the Earth and back for you, for anyone, and you betrayed him – you betrayed us!' I grinded while slowly turning to face her full on.

Danielle was not a crier that's for sure, her eyes and cheeks were lacking that Pal alinseet, or quite simply "The Glow" to be anything but a soft hearted woman. Her reaction to my words spoken were as if Michael had not made it out of that shit hole where there was no telling how many times he would have been beaten, tortured...I didn't want to think about it.

'What, you're blaming me for the shit you got yourself into? That's just rich coming from the likes of you, Lucas Jumped up fucking Cavendish!' Danielle went crazy, really crazy and scary with it, too. If it wasn't for the good timing of Mr. Frobisher walking into the apartment and knocking her out with a single hand chop to the neck, I hate to imagine what she would have done to me.

'GF Sir?' Frobisher asked with his "Wouldn't be the least bit surprised" face.

'That woman Frobisher, is Midnight Blaze, probably the most psychopathic woman in all Resheen. And thank you, by the way. I hope you didn't hit her too hard!'

Asking what it was I was thanking him for, I remarked on the good showmanship of not shooting Miss. La Grande in the back of the head and killing her, and this in turn made the whole matter even more volatile, if not sensitive.

'If it would please My Lord, taking Miss. La Grande to a stop off before appropriately exchanging her would be a great pleasure,' Frobisher mumbled, much to my absolute objection.

'The woman stays with us, do you understand?' I ordered.

He understood perfectly and by acknowledging that he had made an error in judgement of assuming I wanted to dispose of Danielle, he atoned himself to offer his services to any one of us in the apartment, both him and his security team.

'What is the status of our mutual friend?' I asked him looking down at Danielle lying awkwardly on the sofa.

'He is resting peacefully at Safe Haven, Sir, and all but two of the job have been extinguished. May I ask…'

'No. Return home and make our mutual friend comfortable, we have a lot to do it would seem, people to meet, arsehole's to kiss, wars to prevent, you know, that kind of stuff?' I said in a half-sarcastic manner that raised his eyebrow.

Frobisher looked pleased with himself for a quick moment.

'Then it is true, Sir, Evermore and Borello go to war once more?' He asked discreetly..

I looked at him with a dropped stare. 'The two Priests that operated inside Borello and Evermore were from some type of Secret Order breaking into the town…'

'They are The Light, Sir,' Frobisher exclaimed. 'For many years, centuries even, it has been the job of The Illuminati to stand by the construction of the one day perfect Utopian world. Of course, in order to build even a sufficient measure of perfection, you first have to destroy the old world to bring about the new.'

I was amazed by his insight of knowledge, as was Elizabeth, who stepped forward and rearranged Danielle into a more comfortable position of posture.

'Father Benedict was not a part of The Illuminati, he was part of something bigger than a residual Order. The name I was hearing wasn't The Light by any means, it was a New Faith.' Elizabeth told us pointing out of the window and across to The Borello Clock Tower that was lit up, it was as if by some miracle the night had turned into day with the overcast Moon.

It was something that reminded me of an old story my Mother used to read to me when I was younger, the type of story that didn't end with the Prince acquiring the Princess through love and honor, but through the purities vested in ourselves at the time. And then there were the ghost stories, a form of dreadful humor in the hard set mold of Sir. Robert Benson, the fanatic that was running for Evermore Mayor in a few weeks' time.

'Phone ahead of our return please, Mr. Frobisher and have the security doubled night and day. When you have done that I'd appreciate your discretion in making sure Miss. La Grande is escorted safely to Safe Haven, too.' I instructed him of following the instructions to the letter.

Frobisher was not one for defining things in an irritating sleuth kind of way, but his line of questioning was strange in the manner of how he already had the equations worked out before he would suggest anything else.

'Evermore Manor is, at present on Lock Down. It was seen prudent under the circumstances of your wild night out, Sir.' Frobisher informed me with a traitorous look in his eyes.

'How did you do that?' I demanded loudly while grabbing his arm and pulling him away from earshot of the others.

Looking down at my hand grappling him, he looked straight back up and into my face. 'If you don't mind, Sir?' I failed to obey the cries in my head to release him. 'Do what exactly, Sir,' he quipped removing my hand from his arm and flicking imaginary fluff from where it had been. Of course, I took no offense at his strange reaction.

'You knew the whole thing, from start to finish, didn't you, Frobisher? The police who arrived at The Manor, Elizabeth being shot and Danielle coming after me for The Light. You knew that we were going to break Michael out of his Borello Police cell, and without a doubt you know who it is who wants us all dead, too!'

Like a rabbit caught in the headlights, Frobisher broke his stance and gave me a strange look. He was hesitant.

'I'm sorry, Sir, but having served your arrogant, cruel, Potty Mouthed Cousin for so long and having no praise, I found it hard to accept it from you. Those who you wish to discover are not so hard to find when you've served time at Evermore, no offense!'

Offense! I wanted to kick that bastards arse into next week.

'I don't want to fight you, Frobisher, but if I have to…'

'Then surrender, Sir!' Frobisher interjected with a raised hand to the men behind him. 'May I suggest…peacefully?'

It was all fucked up! The run had led me here; three of the town's Most Wanted Assassins: Deadly Night Shade, Midnight Blaze, The Borello Hood, one Northerner and teaspoon of opium that was smashing its potent elixir around my body every which way to Sunday. I was royally screwed.

'Take the women and deliver them to Borello House, as for Lord Cavendish, I will have a few minutes with him alone before we move out.' Frobisher called out without turning away from me. 'Take them now.'

The Guards took a hold of Elizabeth, Danielle and Caterina, their calls to me to do something greeted with a surrender.

'Go with them, don't make this difficult.'

They were taken forcefully from the flat let that only myself and Frobisher now stood in. This was a moment I needed to put a lot of thought into, after all, if I was to go quietly to my death, then the whole of Borello and Evermore would never know the true story of my fall. Personally I wanted to stand.

'I'm sorry, Sir, you were…!'

Before Frobisher could utter another word I had struck out at his throat with an ancient Martial Art move that would see him dead within a couple of seconds, his shock of the move was clear on his face. He didn't even see it coming.

'I'm sorry, too, Frobisher.' I whispered to him as he fell to the floor gasping for air that would never again fill his lungs.

From the flat let I made my way down to the ground floor where I saw the vehicles that Frobisher's men were using, as they also saw me approach, too – alone.

The Master of Guard, Mr. Thompson, stepped from out of the vehicle and looked at me with a slight saddened glance before opening the rear passenger door.

'Evermore, Sir?' He asked.

Nodding my head I climbed inside and sat silent next to Danielle in the back of the car, while Mr. Thompson secured the door and jumped back into the front passenger seat.

'If I may ask, Sir…!'

'No. Have a cleanup detail return and sterilize the area please, Mr. Thompson, and commend your men for a job well done.'

Mr. Thompson nodded with appreciation. Danielle and Elizabeth were now confused as to the situation.

'Frobisher!' Danielle whispered.

'He has joined The Light...he was a good man!'

Elizabeth realized that I had fought with the Staff Hand of Evermore, as did Danielle, who knew only too well that the candidate's The Light hired for their cause, were not easy to defeat – or kill.

Mr. Thompson gave the driver the nod to set off back to the manor house in Evermore, while taking from the dashboard a small dossier that he handed to me.

'Wolf Wake Manor called while you were out, Sir, a Lord Xander O'Neill. There was also a call from a Crystal Lawson of The Light...'

I raised my hand with an almost pestrine wave that silenced him from his briefing, to have him acknowledge the hint of keeping his mouth shut until we reached the manor.

'What do we do now, Lucas?' Danielle asked.

It was time to make decisions, some we would hate, others that we would eventually come around to know and realize were for the best.

'We disappear!' I replied leaning forward and tapping Mr. Thompson on the shoulder

Danielle gave a smile, as did Elizabeth, too. And in unison the two women agreed. The car turned off the road to the 105 and headed straight for Evermore, taking a well-planned detour that took us on the fringes of The Wastelands, a place well known for "The Disappeared". It was here that I managed a brief chuckle before suddenly from out of nowhere our vehicle was blind-sided by another car driving at great speed, both cars now impacted, folded, creased and disintegrated piece by piece. Each window smashed – shattered – while the doors front and back flung open to send Elizabeth, Mr. Thompson and myself out of the rolling vehicle. We had been taken out of The Game...

To Be Continued...!

Casanova Da Vinci

ABOUT THE AUTHOR

Casanova Da Vinci is a twenty-first-century writer of Adult Erotic Literature, some of which may not be suitable for persons under the age of 21-years. It is recommended by both the Author of this work and North Gable Projects (UK), that if anyone comes into contact with this book – Electronic or otherwise, then they should hand it over to an adult. Please respect the advisory stamped by the Author and come back when you have reached the specified age for reading this work.

Thank You

Casanova Da Vinci

To purchase this book up to half-price, then please visit www.gwnonline.com and reserve your copies of the book series: The Bordello Tales.

As to the sequence of these stories, it can be celebrated that the completion run is as so:

Casanova Da Vinci's: Evermore
Casanova Da Vinci's: Midnight Sun
Casanova Da Vinci's: Breathe
Casanova Da Vinci's: Hearts Of Desire
Casanova Da Vinci's: Tears Of The Rain
Casanova Da Vinci's: Living The Quarter Life
Casanova Da Vinci's: The Petticoat Maid
Casanova Da Vinci's: Suburban Heat
Casanova Da Vinci's: Evermore Vs. Borello
Casanova Da Vinci's: Everything Comes To An End

If you have had the opportunity of reading any of the stories so far, then why not follow The Bordello Tales on Casanova Da Vinci's Facebook Page. With Exclusive info, readable books, samples and much more, you'll always be ahead in knowing what's coming up next from this Adult Erotic Author.

Other Books available from North Gable Projects/Suburban Heat Publications (UK):

On A Storyteller's Night Collection

The Brotherhood Of The Realms
On A Storyteller's Night Vol. 1
On A Storyteller's Night Vol. 2

One-Off Mini-Novels:

City Limits: The Long Road Out (2016/2017)
Scarlett (2016/2017)
Vampire Rain (2016/2017)
Angela Morningstar (2016/2017)
Animalistic (2016/2017)

Keep up to date with Casanova Da Vinci's work by Subscribing to:

www.gwnonline.com

1999/2016 © North Gable Projects. All rights reserved

Printed in the USA
CPSIA information can be obtained
at www.ICGtesting.com
CBHW021538211024
16187CB00034B/434